# THE PARADOX OF
# VERTICAL FLIGHT

emil ostrovski

# THE PARADOX OF
# VERTICAL FLIGHT

 **Greenwillow Books,** *An Imprint of HarperCollins Publishers*

Thank you to my parents, who let me spend my summers writing. To my agent, Laura Langlie, for believing in this story. To my editor, Virginia Duncan, and to Tim Smith, managing editor, for helping me make it as strong as possible. To everyone at Greenwillow, who've been so enthusiastic about the book from the very beginning. To Peter, for his incisive feedback. To Jim Clark-Dawe and Kevin Craig, who read the very first draft. To Sylvia Johnson, for her encouragement, enthusiasm, and all those wonderful pep talks. To the folks at Absolute Write, for their support. To my friends, who didn't think I was crazy for wanting to be a writer (or if they did, for keeping it to themselves). To Professor Mitchell Miller, without whose History of Western Philosophy this book may not have been possible, and to the Vassar College Department of Philosophy more generally, for nurturing my interest in a subject that I, like the main character of this novel, love. And, of course, to you, for reading.

The Paradox of Vertical Flight
The text of this book is set in Garamond 3. Book design by Sylvie Le Floc'h

Library of Congress Cataloging-in-Publication Data
Ostrovski, Emil.
The paradox of vertical flight / Emil Ostrovski.
pages cm "Greenwillow Books."
Summary: When, on his eighteenth birthday, Jack Polovsky's almost-suicide is interrupted by his ex-girlfriend Jess's call saying she is in labor, he impulsively snatches the baby and hits the road with his best friend Tommy and Jess to introduce baby Socrates to Jack's aging grandmother.
ISBN 978-0-06-223852-8 (hardback)
[1. Parental kidnapping—Fiction. 2. Babies—Fiction. 3. Fathers and sons—Fiction.
4. Philosophers—Fiction. 5. Automobile travel—Fiction.] I. Title.
PZ7.O8535Par 2013   [Fic]—dc23   2013011911
13 14 15 16 17 LP/RRDH  10 9 8 7 6 5 4 3 2 1
First Edition

 Greenwillow Books

For my grandparents

# THE PARADOX OF
# VERTICAL FLIGHT

# Prologue

The rain blurs the world outside the diner, turns it into a mirage that shifts in the wind and the water and the light. He cradles a cup of hot cocoa in his hands and takes a sip. Our eyes meet, and he smiles—a chocolate-lipped smile. This is his favorite place, despite, or maybe because of, the dirty floors and broken jukebox, a modern diner going for the fifties feel, but sticking with modern prices.

I take an envelope from my coat pocket and slide it over to him.

"For graduation," I say.

"I told you, you didn't have to get me anything," he

says, stressing the "told," and setting the cocoa down on the table for emphasis.

"Yes," I say. "But you didn't mean it. Everyone likes a gift. It means I was thinking about you."

He rolls his eyes and I feel old. When I woke up today, my back hurt, and I thought it must be the weather. Then I thought, My God, I'm attributing my back pain to variations in humidity. I've turned into a cliché. Was I sleeping when this Kafkaesque transformation took place? I must've been, else it would not be properly Kafkaesque. And then I stopped thinking altogether—too much of that particular good thing will leave you a philosopher, and who has the time for such impractical occupations? What do we need philosophy for, when we have airplanes and helicopters, and trains that go 500 miles an hour, or however fast trains go now? I've thought to tell him this, to warn him that the market value for Aristotelian Ethics is near nil, but I know he wouldn't listen.

He insists he wants to study philosophy when he goes off to college, and this, I realize, is largely my fault. Normal fathers do not tell their sons about Socrates and Plato before they can even hold their heads up. What have I led him to? Like Daedalus, I want very much for my son to fly. Like Daedalus, I am afraid he will fall.

"You're worrying," he says. Not a question.

I sigh. Before I can reply, the waitress asks us if we're ready. I order a cheeseburger. He orders a milkshake and fries. Which is ridiculous, the milkshake I mean. It's freezing out there, all he's wearing is his paper-thin Class of '26 T-shirt, and he hasn't even finished his hot chocolate. I wanted to take him out for a decent meal to celebrate his graduation, yet here we sit, waiting on fries and a cheeseburger at a mediocre diner in the middle of a cyclone.

"Diners have good milkshakes," he says, as if that explains everything. Maybe it does. He picks up the envelope. "Would you like me to open it now?"

"No," I say, and mean it. When he sees how much money I've given him, he will give me this pitying look, and it will kill me. "It's just money."

He shrugs. "That's what Mom and Dad gave me."

You'd think I'd be used to it by now. His calling *them* his parents. But I'm not.

"Just don't spend it all on alcohol and drugs and—" "Condoms" is the next word I have in mind, but I can't bring myself to say it. I pick my cocoa up and chug it.

He humors me with a grin, and says, "Cold?"

I nod. Set the cup down. "I have something else for you, too," I say. "A story."

"Oh?" he says, and I think he realizes there's more to my gift than a piece of green paper with a picture of some dead guy on it.

"It's about something that happened to me when I was around your age," I add hurriedly. "It has to do with you."

# 1

## Every Quest Begins With a Call—Or Two

**M**y phone rings, but I don't get up.

In my dream, the teacher hands out frogs, living frogs, and lectures: "Frogs produce smaller air bubbles than humans, who in turn produce smaller air bubbles than llamas. We find this out by drowning the species in question, of course. Please drown your frog and make sure to measure the diameter of its air bubbles, rounding to the nearest significant digit. Tomorrow we'll measure the bubbles produced by our lab partners, and the day after that, the students that are left will move on to the llamas." Some people dream of epic heroes' quests, of saving the universe from a great evil, and I get dreams about the differentiation of air bubbles across species.

Around nine I roll myself into a sitting position, finger the gunk out of my eyes, examine it for a moment, then launch it across the room to where I don't have to immediately deal with it. My roommate's snores filter down from the top bunk.

My cell is on my desk. The blinking red light of a missed call flashes across the room. *Damn.* I missed Bob. I try calling her back, but she doesn't answer. She's always losing her phone, misplacing it; broke it a few times from chucking it, because she couldn't get the *idiotskaya electronica* to work.

I call my grandma "Bob" because I'm too lazy to bother with the alternatives; namely, "Babushka," "Baba," and "*starpur*," the Russian version of old fart. Bob has Alzheimer's, and it's my birthday, so her call means today's one of those days, one of those moments, a flash, when she remembers me.

Partly to distract myself from the guilt, but mostly out of habit, I turn on my computer and wait for Windows to load. I don't capitalize "god" but I always capitalize "Windows." I spend much of my life in front of a screen, plugged into the matrix, looking through a Window into my virtual life. Still waiting on a black dude with a name that sounds like a drug to show up and teach me kung fu, though.

I log in to Facebook and I'm so depressed I want to laugh. Fifteen Facebook friends have wished me a happy birthday so far. I've never really cared about birthdays, honestly—I mean, it's just another day—but to see all these people, most of whom I don't know or in a few years won't remember, wishing me a happy birthday makes me feel like I should care. Like it should be a special day, like it should mean something.

I think I hate Facebook.

I lean back in my chair and stare out the window. When I'm thirty years old, will I still get a bunch of people I don't know wishing me a happy birthday? Will that number dwindle over the years? Will, year by year, some people who've forgotten me remember and some people who've remembered me forget? What's the point of it all, for any of us, if that's the way it goes—if the way it ends is with me logging in to Facebook at ninety years old, bald and fat and wearing a diaper and not remembering how to get to the toilet, which is why I'm wearing a diaper in the first place, and seeing, *what?* Fifteen people I don't know wishing me a happy birthday? And each of my fifteen with fifteen of their own, on and on, a miserable network of Happy Birthday Facebook wishes connecting the entire world, the entire human race, until one day we nuke ourselves and it all goes black and there are no more happy birthdays for anyone.

Sometimes I get like this, depressed I mean, but I'm not one of those crazies, you know, a danger to themselves and others, nothing like that. Never even contemplated suicide, though in a few seconds I will be contemplating jumping out a window. It's hot—seventy, maybe more, my T-shirt's wet on my body, it feels more miserable than it has any right to for a March morning in our great moose-infested state of Maine. I wheel over to open the window, slide it all the way up. I have to stand so I can reach the screen, to slide it down into place. Instead I stick my hand out.

What if I jump? What if I jump, *now?* I don't want to die, but getting hurt would be kind of nice, you know? Like two years ago, when I got my appendix out. Everyone from class sent Get Well cards and Tommy skipped school to spend a day with me playing video games in the hospital. Yeah, that's selfish, but remembering your friend because he almost kicked it is just as selfish.

I turn away from the window. The attention would last a couple weeks, max. Then everyone would go back to their own lives, and everything would be the same. But, unlike when I got my appendix out, I might be crippled for life.

I walk on over to my desk, pull open a drawer, shuffle through video game boxes and CDs and pencils and pens and a worn pink eraser I never use but bring to school every quarter anyway. I grab the bottle of pills, sit back down on my chair, and stare at the bottle. Painkillers. From a few months back, when I got into a fight with a fence over the arbitrary authority by which it goes about the supremely arrogant task of delineating space. The fence won the tiff, but, fractured ankle aside, I'd like to think I'll win the war. I set the painkillers on the desk and check under my bed. That's where I keep my water. There isn't any left, so I stuff the pills in my pocket.

"Hey," comes my roommate Alan's I'm-still-three-quarters-sleeping voice.

I spin around. "Hey," I say, too loud.

He frowns at me, head about three inches off the pillow,

and says, "Feel like I wanted to say something to you. But I forget. I'll remember."

"That's all right."

"Jack," he says, suddenly concerned. "It *is* a Saturday, right?"

"Yeah," I say. "No worries."

"Phew," he says. His head drops back down. Almost every Saturday Alan groggily asks me if it's really the weekend—like he can't quite believe it himself. He's a nice guy, Alan, as nice a roommate as you could hope for, but we don't really do anything together aside from, well, sleeping together. It's just *that* kind of a relationship.

I have my hand on our doorknob when—*voices in the hall.* When they're gone I nudge the door open and head for the bathroom. A guy's in the shower, singing something about how we're meant to be together in a voice that he really should keep a firm leash and a choke collar on if he insists on taking it out in public.

I set the bottle of pills on the shelf below the mirror. My reflection has a zit coming up on his forehead. It hurts to touch. He squeezes anyway, and bites at the inside of his lip. It explodes; a bit of yellow-white pus hits him in the eye and slides down, down, like a tear.

How many pills will kill me and how many will almost kill me? That is the question. It's a fine line, probably. I open the bottle, look inside, frown. Pull the cotton ball out.

I turn on the faucet and hold my hands under the warm water. Close my eyes. Breathe. Breathe. I'm about to down my first pill when my cell rings. Once, twice, three times. The guy in the shower stops singing. I take it out of my pocket.

My breath catches when I see the number.

# 2

## The Sage, the Hero, the Road to McDonald's

Getting to John Bapst's cramped student parking lot is something of an odyssey even on those days when you didn't just get a call from your ex-girlfriend saying she's about to have your kid in some random-ass hospital named after a missionary whose efforts to evangelize the Irish we commemorate once a year by binge-drinking and oh, by the way, Happy Birthday. The parking lot is so far away our student handbook refers to it as being "off campus."

At a traffic light I run into my history teacher, Mr. Jackson, jogging in place while waiting for the "WALK" signal. He nods at me, red-faced and sweaty, and gasps, "Good morning, Mr. Polovsky." I say, "Morning, Mr. Jackson." I could stop him, maybe just talk to him for a few minutes. To give my brain sometime to—I don't know—process. But I don't. I don't like Mr. Jackson much. If only I could take "The World in Antiquity" with Mr. Fox all over again, instead of Jackson's boring-ass US/local history that makes me want to drink hemlock.

Case in point: last semester, Mr. Jackson made us pick a local event of major historic significance to write a research paper on. This was something of a paradoxical assignment, as nothing of "major historic significance" has ever taken place in Maine, much less Bangor. I thought and thought, and finally decided to do my paper on our first lawsuit, in 1790, in which a Mr. Buswell sued a Mr. Wall after the latter called the former "an old damned gray-headed bugger of Hell." Mr. Jackson had written "Cute, Mr. Polovsky," and given me a B-minus. Apparently, you get marked down for cuteness. After all, John Bapst Memorial is a serious academic institution devoted wholeheartedly to the intellectual development of its pupils. Our motto is "Integrity, Achievement, Respect" for Christ's sake! This is not the sort of place where you can make a joke of your research paper and *not* get a B-minus. How could I possibly have expected less from the school that produced the wife of Stephen King?

Wait. How can I be thinking about my B-minus last semester WHEN I'M ABOUT TO HAVE A KID? AND WHAT DOES TABITHA KING HAVE TO DO WITH *ANYTHING*?

At my car I fumble with the keys. Then I'm in, and driving. When I told her she should get an abortion she told me she never wanted to see me or my little pecker again. I thought this was a low blow and said she was acting like it was that special time of the month. She screamed, "No, you idiot, I'm pregnant," and threw a chair at me. She threw a goddamn chair at me. Did I let that stop me? No. I left a million messages. Showed up, I don't know, like a dozen times. And what did she do? She told me it was none of my business anymore and threw *another chair* at me. Now she wants me back. For what? So we can start a jolly old family together? So she can make me watch as she gives my kid away for adoption? *Fuck that shit.*

Half an hour later, I'm at Jess's bedside and Doctor Winters, a gray-mustached little man with a brown stain on his coat, is saying, "Young man, you must be the father. What's your name?"

"No," Jess says. "No. He's—its—he's just Jack. A friend. I guess."

I smile awkwardly at the doctor and he smiles awkwardly at me. He gives us a nod, clears his throat, and says, "Well. Jack and Jess. I'll give you two a few minutes alone, then. Call if you need anything."

Then we're alone.

"Everyone else I know is either drunk, on vacation, or dead," she says, and sniffs.

"Oh," I say, looking at her enormous belly. I did this to her. I . . . did this to her. And then she threw two chairs at me. Not at the same time. Probably a couple months apart. *Still.* Two chairs. Or rather, the same chair, two times.

"And it's your birthday, and his birthday—what're the odds of that?—so I figured maybe—" She leaves the thought unfinished.

"Three-sixty-five times three-sixty-five," I tell her.

"—what?"

"Three-sixty five times three-sixty-five. Three-sixty-five squared. That's—those are the odds."

When she doesn't respond, I keep talking. I need to fill the space between us with words. "How are you going to, you know, take care of it with school and all?" My thoughts are everywhere: *St. Patrick's? Really? What kind of hospital names itself St. Patrick's?* And *if you have half a brain you'll give the kid up for adoption*, and *But shouldn't I get to have a say in that decision?* And *I'm not sure I want to give it up for adoption,* and *Does that mean I don't have half a brain?* and . . .

She looks at me, hard. "I'm giving him up for adoption," she says. "Already met the family. Just have to sign."

"Him?" I ask.

"Yes." A tear runs down her face. I turn away.

A long silence follows. I say, "I'm sorry," in a soft voice. I'm not sure she even hears me. When she finally breaks the silence, it is with a long moan.

Waiting room. The room where we wait. The room where I sit, with my legs crossed, and then uncrossed. Where the lady on one side of me talks loud on her phone, but I can't get too mad at her—she's crying, crying to her sister or her mother or whomever. She has the volume of her phone turned up so loud I hear both sides of the conversation, except for the times when her sobs drown out whoever's on the other end. Why is she here alone? Why is she *waiting* alone?

The boy to my left—no more than eight years old, his

feet don't even reach the floor—looks warily from me to his mother, to me again, and asks, "You're waiting for someone too? I'm waiting for my brother." I open my mouth to explain. Nothing comes out. Finally I say, "I'm waiting for my friend. My friend's in there, and she's having a baby. And I'm waiting for her." Though I don't want to hear, though I really don't want to hear, I ask the boy "Is your brother okay?"

"He took too many pills. On accident. Too much medicine is bad for you."

I nod. *Yes.* Yes, it is.

I make a list of all the things that could go wrong.

• The baby could be stillborn.

• Jess could have complications. Jess could die.

• The baby could be stillborn.

• Jess could have complications. Jess could die.

• The baby could be stillborn. The baby could be stillborn. And Jess . . .

A nurse passes by, and I get up, ask her, "Do you know where the vending machines are?" She points and says, "Down that hall right there, by the bathrooms."

What a nice place to keep the food.

I even laugh a little, though it's not funny.

At the vending machines I stand awhile, and my mind drifts to the party where I met Jess.

*I nod at a guy dry-humping the couch a few feet away and say, "Classy party, huh?"*

*She follows my gaze and shrugs. "Party's a party. Only thing that varies is the quality of the alcohol."*

*"I don't really even like alcohol," I say, looking at the drink in my hand. Piss in a cup could probably pass for beer. In terms of appearance* and *taste.*

*"Me neither," she says.*

*"But being drunk is kinda fun," I say with a grin.*

*"I'll drink to that," she says, and raises her own cup of piss. We clink.*

A man exits the nearby bathroom and I feel suddenly self-conscious. I get M&Ms and a Coke and return to my seat. The damn M&Ms won't open, and sometimes, sometimes the umbilical cord strangles a baby before it's born, the baby gets wrapped up in it and turns blue.

I feel a tap on the shoulder. A nurse. Her smile. She's smiling.

"Your friend is fine," she tells me. "She and the baby are fine. They're resting. We'll want to keep the mother here awhile, just to make sure everything's all right. If you'd like, you can follow me and I'll bring you to them."

I remain sitting.

"Can you just—I think I need a minute. I—umm, I'd like to finish my M&Ms."

That's what I tell her. "I'd like to finish my M&Ms."


The first M&M is green: Early October. We hadn't spoken in two weeks. Jess called, asked me to come over.

Brown: I drove to her dorm thinking *she's going to break up with me.* Fun was had during the summer, I would know, I was there, after all, but with her friends back on campus, she didn't need some kid who hadn't even taken the SATs yet hanging around anymore. *People move on. C'est la vie, Jacky-boy. Learn some French for Christ's sake. All her consensual-age "college" friends probably know French.*

Green: Actually, Dan-the-swimmer was a classics major. Taking Advanced Latin that semester, the douche.

Orange: And then there was Carol.

Brown: Carol had a major in prelaw. She intended to go to law school (Columbia, to be precise, the facilities were apparently to her liking) to learn law. Which meant her four years of undergrad would be spent—what—studying the "pre" part of "prelaw"? I just didn't get it.

Blue: "Jack, sometimes I get the feeling you don't like my friends."

Blue: "Jack, sometimes I get the feeling you're jealous."

Yellow: "I don't know what you're talking about Jess. Your friends are—*fabulous*."

"Fabulous?"

"Fabulous."

"I might believe you if not for the fact that I've never heard you call anything fabulous. Ever."

"Don't be ridiculous. I call things fabulous all the time."

"And the expression on your face—"

"My dear, that's the face I make when I'm with you. If you don't like it—"

"No darling, that's the face you make when you're taking shots of cheap vodka *with me.*"

"I—*love*—cheap vodka."

Red: "She's a *prelaw* major, Jess. I mean, Christ, not to be judgmental or anything but that's almost as bad as communications."

"Not everyone gives a shit about Nietzsche and infinite return, Jack. In fact, it might be just you."

"Eternal return."

"What?"

"It's *eternal* return."

"Whatever."

Brown: We'd called or texted or Facebooked every day during the summer. How had we come to this? First bickering, then a *two-week* silence complete with imaginary tumbleweeds rolling through the metaphorical desert wasteland of our relationship. Of course she was breaking up with me. I blamed Dan.

Red: When I got to her room, she sat down with me on her bed, wouldn't meet my eye. She started telling me how in bio lab that day she'd dissected a frog. "Inside the frog, Jack, there were all these—so many—eggs. I talked to the professor after class. Frogs can lay up to thirty thousand eggs at a time. Did you know that?"

Orange: I didn't know what to say to this. In my head I'd been rehearsing my "Farewell, you bitch" speech, because it hurt, the thought of her breaking up with me. I thought I loved Jess; sometimes when we held hands or plain old talked, nothing big, for no reason I'd feel so *excited,* so god-damn fucking excited just being close to her. I didn't know if that was the "love" everybody talks so much about, but I didn't want to give it up—her, the feeling, love, lust, chemicals doing a jig in my brain, whatever—and so I was going to make our parting of ways as difficult as possible. But instead of breaking up with me she went off and gave me a dissertation on *frogs*. And proceeded to regard me with such expectation, like it was so painfully obvious to her how I ought to respond.

Yellow: "It's probably because of the mortality rate," I managed.

"What?"

"The mortality rate," I said. "I mean, thirty thousand probably sounds like a lot, but I bet only a tiny percentage of those frogs would have ever grown into adults and gone on to reproduce."

Silence. Then, "Jack?"

"Yeah?"

"You're an asshole."

"What?"

"You're a fucking asshole. A goddamn fucking asshole. A gigantic—"

"Hey, I mean, I'm not the one who went and killed the frog. You're the one who—"

"Jack, I'm pregnant."

"—split her open to draw her small intestine."

We stared at each other.

"Sorry?" I finally croaked.

Brown: It was like she'd been waiting for the signal and I'd just unwittingly given it. It amazed me how quickly Jess's voice grew so loud and went so high. I got enough to understand that my insensitivity to the plight of frogkind was only the most recent in a long series of wrongs. "Didn't I ask you if you put the damn rubber on right? Didn't I say 'Jack, that looks a little off?' Didn't I say that? Didn't you tell me it was fine? You'd done it before. Wink wink. Nudge nudge. Ha ha. *'Not like I haven't done this before.'* Well I guess it was a little off, *Jack*—and now I'm a little pregnant, a little knocked up, have a little bun in my little oven—what am I going to do? What am I even going to do? I was waiting for you to *call.* I've been wanting to tell you—two weeks already. And now you're only here after *I* called *you*, practically told you to get your ass over here, but nothing's changed, nothing's fixed, surprise fricking surprise," and finally, she said with a half-sob, "I know it's superficial, but I don't want to be fat."

Green: I looked at her with wide eyes and said the only words that I could think of. "It's going to be okay."

Green: She reached over, grasped her pillow with one

immaculately manicured hand, and smacked me in the face with it. And again.

Putting my hands up, I said, "Ow—Jess! What the hell! You got me in the eye that time!"

"Oh, did I? Did I get you in your eye? I'm so *sorry!*" She swung again. "*It's going to be okay.* It's going to be *okay?* Easy for you to say! You can just hit and run!"

"What?"

"You heard me. I'm surprised you didn't run off the second I told you."

Blue: Her words sank in. She kept it to herself for two weeks, waiting for me . . .

"You didn't tell anyone? Anyone else?"

The arm holding the pillow relaxed a bit. "No."

Red: "I don't know how you did it, Jess," I said, and gave her a weak smile. "If I got pregnant and had to keep quiet about it for two weeks—I would—I don't know."

Orange: Jess let the pillow drop. "You pregnant would be a nightmare. You're already so *needy*."

"Don't be ridiculous. I am *not* needy."

"Oh, yeah, you are."

"No, I'm not."

Brown: "Admit it, Jack. It was your wounded sense of masculine pride that kept you from picking up the damn phone."

"My masculine pride has nothing to do with anything. Though I'm not going to lie, I'm of the opinion that a girlfriend shouldn't laugh when her boyfriend loses in an arm-wrestling match—"

"I *knew* it—"

"And besides, Dan cheated."

"How is that, Jack? How does one cheat at arm-wrestling?"

"By having like fifty pounds on me—"

"You were arm-wrestling, Jack, not sumo-wrestling—"

"Yeah, well, his arm weighs more than mine, and why are we even talking about this?"

Blue: Jess sighs. "Because, Jack. Because where you and me, where we stand matters more than anything right now. I didn't tell anyone else, because I knew what they'd say. They'd tell me I shouldn't have it—the baby."

"Jess," I said, my throat dry, "you're not actually thinking of keeping it, are you?"

"What do you mean I'm not actually thinking of keeping it?"

I froze up. Barely managed to say, "You can't have it, Jess—"

She laughed then, made me jump. "*Excuse* me? You of all people, I thought would—but why am I surprised? You're too young. I've always known it."

"You're like two years older than me—"

"Three, Jack. And I guess that's more of a difference than I kept telling myself it was."

"W-what does my age have to do with anything? I mean . . ." I paused. Statistics about kids our age with children flew through my head, their chances of graduating college, getting decent jobs, their chance at normal life.

"While I'm still young," she said.

"That's just it, Jess. We're both too young. For this."

"Do you love me?"

I opened my mouth, closed it. I *did* love her. Or at least, I thought I did. But I couldn't tell her, couldn't bring myself to say "yes." I didn't have enough air in my lungs to utter that one stupid, monosyllabic word. So I just stared at her, dumb and ashamed.

She turned away. I wanted to touch her, to whisper the word I couldn't say over and over again into her ear, with her hair in my face and the warmth of her pressed against me.

But every time I tried, I pictured some wrinkly little monster with a load in its pants and the rest of my life laid out for me—the baby's first steps, first word, which obviously wouldn't be "Dad," first day of school, first car, high school graduation, marriage, a kid, aka my grandkid, oh Christ my grandkid, wrinkly little monster with a load in its pants the sequel, how *old* would I be by then—and I just couldn't.

"Jess—I—is this the best time? For this?"

"It's the only time, Jack," she said, her voice sad. She looked at me and said, "Do you love me?"

And I said, "I don't know."

And she said, "You need to leave then."

And I said, "Jess, I really think you shouldn't have it."

"Jack, just go—"

"Listen to me, Jess, will you please just listen—" That was the moment I almost told her: I love to hate the parties, because I get to hate them with you and sometimes when you talk I don't listen, because I like to watch your lips move and most of all I like to watch your eyes—you can't listen and watch someone's eyes at the same time. It's like trying to watch porn on the computer while talking on the phone with your best friend Tommy—it just doesn't work. And I wanted to tell her that once when I got drunk *and* high and felt like my body was melting I thought if we ever had kids (someday far, far in the future) they would be really cute, mostly thanks to her, and when that day (far, far in the future) came I wouldn't give a flying, walking, or commuting-by-train shit how fat she got, since eyes always stay the same regardless of your waistline or how saggy and Silly Putty-like your breasts get.

She interrupted me, though. She said, "No, Jack, I think I've heard enough. I think I've heard enough about what I can't do and the babies I can't have. I'd like you to go now." She drew a deep breath. "Don't call. I don't want to see you or your little dick again."

"Jess, you're acting like it's that special time of the month."

Her eyes narrowed. She had her hand on this foldout beach chair she uses with her desk; she always insisted it's the most comfortable chair ever. "No, you idiot, I'm pregnant!" A half second later I discovered another of the chair's remarkable properties; its surprisingly aerodynamic character.

Yellow: Driving back to my dorm, I pictured those thirty thousand frogs hatching from the same mother, then growing, living, and dying, in thirty thousand different places and thirty thousand different ways, with only a few having lived long enough to lay thirty thousand eggs of their own, and so the circle continues, on and on it goes, until all the stars in the universe go out. I pulled over, called Jess, wanting to talk to her about the frogs, about all those little frogs.

She wouldn't pick up.

I do my best to avoid looking at our son—oh god, our *son*—and ask the only question that I can think of. "How—how are you doing?"

"How am I doing," she repeats. *"How am I doing?* Oh I don't know, Jack. A nine-pound bundle of joy just pushed his way out of my uterus. He looks a little like you and me and I'm about to give him away. But other than that I'm fucking fantastic."

Silence.

Finally she sighs, then says, "Would you like to hold him?"

This is her revenge. For the way I acted when she first told me. *Here, Jack. Hold your son, and then watch me give him away.*

"Okay," I say, real quiet, and take a few tentative steps forward.

She holds him out, her gaze averted. I take him like she's handing me a bundle of C4, my arms trembling. I hold him to my chest. He's so light, so soft. What if I drop him? I sit down on the edge of the bed and close my eyes. He breathes into my neck. In my head I sing him a lullaby.

"The parents are here," Jess is saying. "They're going to take him away now. Any minute. I know it's for the best, but—"

"Do you hear how he's breathing? He's—it's kind of uneven. Like he stops every so often. Jess—"

"Jack, are you even listening to me?"

"Jess, I'm saying his breathing." I'm a bit panicked now. My heart thumps madly. "His breathing—it's kind of uneven—"

"They say they all breathe like that, Jack," she says, exasperated. "*Listen to me*—"

"Are you sure? Maybe we can ask—"

"They all fucking breathe like that, Jack!" She's crying. When did she start crying?

She rolls over, pulls a pillow over her face, and mumbles something through it.

"What?" I say.

This time I make her words out. "Just go. Both of you. Give him to a nurse and go."

I'm at the door when she says in that half-muffled voice, "Happy fucking birthday."

I exchange a few words with a nurse who nods with such sympathy, I'm surprised her spinal column remains intact. My head is reeling and I don't know if I'm making much sense: "I'm—Jess—my friend asked me to—" I pause, unsure of how to continue. Gesturing with the baby in my arms, I say, "She—Jess, I mean—wants me to give him to you to give to them. The parents, I mean . . . But I haven't signed anything. Do I need to sign something?"

She puts a warm hand on my shoulder. "Honey, my name is Nurse Illard. You can call me Mary. We'll figure everything out, okay? Now what's all this about you not signing anything? The mother's the only one who needs to sign, honey, since the father's unknown."

Unknown. The father is unknown.

"Honey, are you okay?" she asks, concern on her face. "Would you like me to take him? I'll bring him to his new parents. They're a lovely couple."

"The Father's not unknown," I say.

"What?"

"The Father's not unknown," I say, louder. I'm shaking a little. *What am I doing?* "I'm the father."

The nurse regards me with wide eyes. "Are you sure?"

I nod. "Can I just—have a few minutes with him? Alone? Just a couple. Minutes."

She gives me a strange look. Hesitates. "I'm sorry, the mother clearly stated," she says, shaking her head. "You'll need to go back to the mother's room. I'll bring the doctor along and we'll get everything sorted out, okay?" She smiles. I try to smile back.

"Okay," I say, and I start to head back in the direction of Jess's room, but I can't. I can't go back in there. Jess will *literally* leap out of bed and murder me. Besides. All I want is a minute or two. Just to hold him, and to think. I wipe my brow with my free hand. It comes away slick with sweat. I glance behind me—Nurse Illard's hurrying off in another direction. I pass Jess's room and keep going, down the hallway, nurses and doctors bustling past me. On my right, an empty room. I duck inside, and shut the door.

I pace back and forth and almost forget I'm carrying the baby against my shoulder until I see our translucent reflections in the window. I set the bugger on the bed and frown at him. He looks at me for a few seconds in this cross-eyed sort of way. At least, I think he's looking at me. Or maybe it's just his nose. Actually I'm pretty sure he's just really interested in his nose. It's a pretty great nose, as far as noses go. I did that much for him.

I pick him up again. I should feel something, some biological, evolutionary outpouring of love . . .

*She didn't even ask me.*

Even when I got to the hospital, she didn't ask what I wanted or how I felt. Just "I'm giving him up for adoption." Granted, I had not wanted him in the first place . . . I had not wanted him, but now he's here, and he has my nose, my goddamn nose. He has it now, and he'll have it after I'm gone.

What else does he have? What other parts of me will live on after I'm dead?

I can't give him up.

The thought frightens me. I try to push it away. It returns, harder, more insistent.

*I can't give him away.* Not *yet.* I wrap the baby in the bed-sheet, turning him into a white cocoon. Too tight? Can I take him out of the room just like that? *No.* No, no, no. What if I run into Nurse Illard? Around his ankle is a little metal brace-let that I'm pretty sure will set off every alarm in Maine the second I take so much as a step in the wrong direction.

I wipe at my sweaty forehead again, and tell myself to think.

Think. *Think.*

I catch our reflections in the window again. Catch them and laugh.

I cross the room in a rush. The window's unlocked, it's only a short drop, three feet or so, but I have to hurry.

I clamber through awkwardly. Glance over my shoul-der, expecting someone to race out after me, for alarms to blare and loudspeakers to declare they have a ten-twenty-three-and-a-half plus forty on their hands. It doesn't feel right, that stealing a baby should be so easy. Fucking random-ass hospital. What if it had been my baby? But then, it is. Or is it? My heart says yes, the law says no. Or does it? Maybe the more prudent course of action would have been of the legal, as opposed to illegal, variety. Bit late for that.

At my car. Any moment they're going to figure out the baby is gone. His blue eyes meet mine with a look of reproach.

"I'm sorry—" I pause, unsure what to call him. Mate? Buddy? Man? Dude? Dudeling? *Sonny?* No. Still, I have to call him something. And then, suddenly, I remember the name I gave my brother.

My parents never named him. They didn't want to get too attached, but I knew it would work. It had to. It was meant to be, we were meant to be, him and me. Besides, how complicated could it be? Fertilize egg. Implant egg. A two-step procedure that our insurance didn't fully cover and that put my parents thousands into debt. For me. Because I asked them to.

Mom was pregnant for a week before she broke the news to me. Three weeks later she lost him. She hadn't named him, but I had. It was a joke. We'd been eating dinner. I brought up baby names. My parents both gave me a don't-start look, but I nevertheless bulldozered on and suggested—Socrates. Ha. Ha. Ha. Sometimes I kill myself.

"Look, Socrates," I say, swatting the tears from my eyes. "I'm sorry for kidnapping you. And for—" My stomach lurches. I don't want to say it. "And for not wanting you. I was just really, really scared. But I'm going to figure it all out. First though—first we need to *move.*"

I start walking. I can't drive, no safety seat or anything.

Where the hell would I put him? The glove compartment? A minute or two later, right where the parking lot meets the street, I still have no idea where I'm going, but wherever it is I'm getting there slow. I kneel down, careful, and take out my phone. Scroll through contacts. Find CAB. Click Talk.

"Yeah, hullo? Al's Taxi."

"Hi. Umm—"

"*Hullo?* This here's Al's Taxi. If you got me on speaker phone take that off, never hear a damn thing—"

"Sorry, I need, there's a McDonald's by St. Patrick's—"

"Need a cab or asking me on a fancy date? I'm happily married but, eh, that never stopped no one—*ha.* Kidding, keep them pants on, son. You're not my type. Be there in fifteen."

"Sorry, I, uh, I need a baby seat as well. Can you—are you there? Are you—"

"Yeah yeah, baby seat, got it, got tons of them lying around. Practically swimming in baby seats here, son."

I hang up. Cars race past us and the sun rises higher and higher overhead. I'm sweaty, Socrates is sweaty. He's crying. I might be, too.

What am I doing?

# 3

## Over the Hills and Far Away in a Cab

The cab isn't there when we get to the McDonald's, so I call again. The cabbie picks up on the fourth ring with an irritated, *"Hullo?"*

"Hi. This is—I just called you a few minutes ago. I'm at the McDonald's now—"

"Look, I don't got a jet here. If I had a jet I'd be there now. But I haven't got round to getting my pilot license. Or a jet."

"All right, sorry, just wanted to make sure."

I go inside the McDonald's and get in line. My arm's numb from carrying Socrates (all nine pounds of him), who's still crying. Everyone inside looks at me like I should do something. I pretend not to notice. It's really pretty amazing how much noise can come out of something so small.

When the girl working the register—after some hesitation—asks me what I want, I say a Big Mac meal, a Coke, and applesauce. But then, didn't I read not too long ago about how drinking Coke gives you a fifty-seven-percent greater chance of growing an extra head or whatever? I'm a father now, so I switch to a water. The girl doesn't understand about being a father, she's too young even though she looks older than me. She doesn't say anything, just rolls her eyes and takes her revenge on the machine.

She can't get it right, so she calls the manager, and the manager is a forty-year-old guy, squat and short, who's going bald and has this pathetic McDonald's T-shirt that says "I'm lovin' it." He doesn't look like he's lovin' it at all.

He gets it right and all I want to do is stay in that nice air-conditioned interior, but Socrates is still bawling so I sit at one of the tables they have outside, like an exile, and lay my son down next to my food. I unwrap him like he's a taco. Even before I finish I know what's inside this taco and though it's vaguely greenish, it's *definitely* not guacamole. I reach for the napkins included with my meal and initiate

Operation Anus Wipe, but I'm distracted by this plastic blue clip right where his belly button should be. It makes me nauseous. I give it a gentle poke.

I wouldn't have thought it possible, but he starts crying even harder, as if to say *you're doing it all wrong, Dad*, and I want to say, "If I crapped myself and had a plastic clip through my belly-button I'd be mad, too." I don't, as that's not a very fatherly thing to say. To make matters worse, Operation Anus Wipe runs into logistical problems of the they-didn't-give-me-enough-napkins variety. I wipe my hands on the sheet.

What to do. What to do. McDonald's. Bathrooms. *Baby-changing stations.* I feel like Archimedes after he discovered the displacement of water. Instead of running around naked screaming, "Eureka!" I pick up naked baby Socrates, go inside, and take him to the bathroom.

Once my hands are clean and I have Socrates wrapped in a brand-new toilet-paper diaper, we go back outside. I try to feed him some applesauce. Mostly I just get it all over his face.

"Look, buddy, it's a plane," I tell him.

He looks at me like I'm an idiot.

"It's a plane," I insist.

Or maybe he's just looking at his nose again.

When the taxi finally comes I scoop Socrates up in one hand, grab the bag containing the rest of my meal in the other, and make for the passenger-side door. Once inside, I see he has not brought a baby seat to the tune of "Over the Hills and Far Away."

I ask him if it's in the trunk, and he says "What?" and I say "The baby seat," and he repeats, "The baby seat," in a tone that suggests he'd sooner have a dead body stashed in the trunk than a baby seat, even though I expressed no interest whatsoever in dead bodies.

"The baby seat I asked you to bring. On the phone you told me—"

"Look, son, do I look like Babies R Us to you? I got no baby seat." With that, he starts driving. "So where we goin'?"

"The nearest ATM. That would be great."

"Look, son," he says, "I'm not Google Earth here. Do I look like Google Earth? I don't do nearest this, nearest that. You know the place—specific, right?—then you tell me, and I go. Otherwise you can go on your way." He scoffs. "Nearest this nearest that."

So I tell him a place, a *specific* place, and we ride in

silence until I get the courage to ask our driver if he knows what babies eat, aside from formula.

"What?" he says in that same corpse-in-the-trunk tone.

"Do you—umm, know what babies eat?" I ask, louder this time.

"Do I know what babies eat?" he repeats, and laughs. "Yeah, I know," he says. "I got three of them monstrosities at home, why you think I work Saturdays, eh?"

"Well?" I ask.

"Well," he says. "Well they got these, these little containers, little ones for babies, Gerber or I-don't-know." He brings up both hands from the wheel to show me how itty-bitty the containers are and I want to tell him to keep his hands on the wheel. "But the real little one," he says, "all he does is suck his ma's tit dry."

He laughs at this and I smile, but then he asks in a gruff voice, "You think that's funny, eh? You think there's something funny 'bout my wife's dry tits, they're something to be smirking about, eh? 'Cause if you do maybe I just pull over and drop you on the side of the road. Yeah, I'm working on a Saturday, but that don't mean I got to take this crap on my day off."

My smile quickly fades.

• • •

At the Walmart Supercenter, I tell the cabbie to wait, and, turning on the radio, he says "Sure, son, I'll wait all day. Meter's running, though."

I head straight for the ATM. Getting my wallet out of my pocket and my card out of my wallet while holding a baby is a feat and a half, but the people behind me are too busy being too-busy-for-this-line to applaud. I swipe my debit card and it says "card not recognized." I swipe it again, and it says "card not recognized." The woman behind me tells me I'm swiping it the wrong way even though the diagram is approximately three point six inches from my face and I am doing it the way it shows. I try again, my way, and it says "card not recognized." The lady behind me emits this clucking noise. What the hell, might as well try it *her* way. It gives me a different sort of error message with a bunch of numbers and letters.

*Damn.* I should probably back away very slowly . . .

A man clears his throat and then there's that clucking again. I want to do violent things to lady-clucks-a-lot, but I am a father now, so I restrain myself. Right then my phone starts vibrating. I've got Socrates in one hand, my useless debit card in the other, and my pants are shaking from the vibrate, and I actually kind of want to stand there for a while, just like that, because the vibrate feels kind of good. Instead I step away from the ATM, slide my card into my pocket and my phone out of it, flip it open, say hello, and hear:

"Where the fuck is my baby?"

I remain silent and dumb for about half a second, then flip it closed, and stuff it back into my pants. A few seconds later it rings again. This time I don't answer.

*Her* baby. The one she was about to give away. *Her* baby. I try to banish her from my mind.

I look around the Walmart. Everywhere, old women and young women and little girls race grocery carts, back them up, do three-point turns and U-turns, cross into the opposite lanes, ignore the implied traffic signals, run over feet and into other carts, all while the men grumble to themselves and shuffle about like zombies without a human to chase. The senior citizens lean on carts and push onward, inch by inch, staring wide-eyed and with half-open mouths at the sheer speed of life. All this movement proves too much even for me and my young bladder.

In the bathroom, my options are grim. I can set Socrates down in the sink, pee, and hope he doesn't fall out or drown or that someone else doesn't kidnap him while I relieve myself. I can hold him while I pee, but I am not sure I possess the manual dexterity to unzip my fly, pull down my boxers, pull up my pecker, calculate the proper trajectory, angle to compensate for the fact that I slept on said pecker the wrong way last night (from the look of it this morning), and fire, all while holding my son and making sure he does not look down, since I'm sure seeing where you came from on Day One is one-hundred-three percent guaranteed to seriously mess you up or your money back.

I choose the first option, and wait for the bathroom to clear out so as not to draw too much attention to myself, but quickly see that's not going to happen. If anything, the bathroom seems more densely populated than the rest of the store, as if everyone comes to Walmart Supercenter not to shop but to gawk at their toilet facilities. To join a line of strange men guarding their urinals like sentinels and pretend, with the greatest degree of stern concentration, that the other men do not exist and that you are not the least bit curious as to whether your cannon packs more firepower than the one belonging to that guy over there (who, incidentally, does not exist).

A kid about three years younger and as many inches

taller shoulders past me and says, "Hey. Hey creepy guy with the baby. You two peeping or what?"

"We're *thinking*," I say.

I pick a sink and set Socrates in it. I walk over to an unoccupied urinal, but crane my head so I can watch Socrates's sink. Someone from beyond my field of vision says, "Aw, shit. I think I'm—*shit*. Not *again*. Anyone else here see a baby in a sink? Anyone?"

"He's mine," I call, as I relieve myself.

"Why the hell'd you put him in a sink then?"

"He felt like it was the place to be," I say, as I wash my hands.

"Fair enough," the man says. "Never thought about it from his perspective."

"Yeah, well," I say, grab Socrates, and head back into the store to find the baby aisle, where my pants promptly start vibrating again.

At the far end of the aisle are some of those carry-around-like-a-basket cribs. I pull one down, and as I lay Socrates inside I'm surprised to see he's dozing. I take my cell out—two missed calls and a bunch of texts, all from Jess. I almost call her back, but . . . maybe the FBI or whoever is listening in and just waiting to get me talking for five seconds or whatever so they can put a trace on my location and have SWAT teams dropping in through the ceiling of Walmart to arrest me in the baby aisle.

I opt for texting.

I type out *Socrates and I are fine.* Hit Send. Realize she doesn't know I named the baby. I get a text back: *JACK PICK UP THE FUCKING PHONE AND ARE YOU FUCKING INSANE/ON DRUGS*

And another: *WHO THE FUCK IS SOCRATES*

And another: *WHERE IS MY BABY*

My phone is vibrating again. I turn off the sound *and* the vibrate. Just for a few seconds, so I can close my eyes and think.

Nice and calm. Nice and calm, nice and calm, nice and calm, but it's not nice and calm. I've stolen a fricking baby. I imagine my yearbook picture plastered on the wall of some police captain's office—the one from last year, where I look like I smoked weed for a week before having it taken—and alerts going up on the radio and television to be on the lookout for a delusional, drugged-up teenager who has kidnapped a baby, believing him to be a two-thousand-year-dead philosopher.

Well, you know what? Socrates has been dead for much

more than two thousand years, closer to twenty-four hundred. Why am I not surprised the media can't get even the most basic facts right? But then—this particular media broadcast is of the imaginary sort, so it is actually *I* who am to blame for this campaign of misinformation.

I open my eyes with the intention of keeping them open for the foreseeable future.

*Concentrate, Jack.*

Supplies, I need supplies, and the cabbie's waiting . . .

I grab the first baby bottle I see. It's a start.

I get in line at one of those five-items-or-less checkouts, behind a grandpa who must have added a zero or three to the five. A few minutes later, diapers, a bottle, baby formula, a blanket, some clothes, and a baby in a basket roll in single file toward a middle-aged cashier—*Candice*. I almost took some regular old milk, but managed to remember, literally, the only two things I learned in Home Ec class:

Gravity is a baby's worst enemy. Even when the baby is a potato.

Babies can't digest regular milk. Not even goat's milk, which has a terribly misleading picture of a baby on its carton.

The grandpa lingers, receipt held so close to his eyes

he can probably make out individual molecules. Candice manages to scan the diapers and bottle before he says, "Excuse me."

"Yes," Candice says.

"Excuse me, but I believe you charged me for three boxes of oatmeal cookies. I bought four."

"I'll be with you in a moment, sir," she says.

"Oh, of course," the grandpa says, as if seeing me for the first time. He gives me a golden-toothed smile. I smile back. He must be at least eighty, or more. Born before computers and television. Back when times were simple and Coca-Cola still had cocaine in it. Will *I* recognize the world when my turn to bother cashiers with questions about oatmeal cookies comes along? Maybe it has nothing to do with the oatmeal cookies at all. Maybe this cashier is the only person grandpa will talk to all day.

Candice frowns at my baby-in-a-basket and clears her throat. "There's a sale on, buy a basket, get a baby at half off," I tell her.

Candice doesn't laugh. Grandpa nods in agreement, says, "That's how I got mine," and begins to shuffle around in his wallet while muttering. "Have a coupon—in here—somewhere—sure I do, sure I do."

"You'll have to remove the baby before I can scan the basket, sir," Candice tells me.

"I just *know* it's here," the grandpa says.

"Sir," Candice insists.

"Somewhere, got to be somewhere—" the Grandpa says.

I pick Socrates up, Candice scans the basket, and I pay for everything with what little cash I have on me. On my way out, I turn back to the grandpa. Tell him, "Have a nice day," and he says, "Oh, yes, it already is," and then I leave him to his coupons and his oatmeal cookies.

The cab is miraculously still waiting. Before the driver can come up with some wiseass remark I say, "Pull into that Mobil down the road a bit. I'm pretty sure they have an ATM."

"I thought you came *here* for an ATM."

"Just go, please."

"Whatever, son, long as you got the money, I'll drive you sightseeing to every ATM machine in the country." Then he seems to make the connection between ATM machines and money, and says, "You do have the money, don't you?"

"Yeah," I say.

We pull into the Mobil station and I get out, taking Socrates with me.

"Hey—son, you can leave the baby with me. No need to drag the little monster round and round."

"Uh, no, thank you."

I set the basket down on the floor by the ATM machine, slide in my card, and what do you know? It actually lets me withdraw my money.

In the parking lot, I pull open the cab door to find the driver talking on his cell. He says, "I've got to go now. Okay. Bye." To me, "Where to now?"

"You can just—I'll give you directions as we go. Make a right out of the station—"

He doesn't argue. Says, "Whatever you say, man."

I'm suspicious, but the only bright idea I have is bailing out of the car. This, aside from being logistically difficult, would probably also be a bit of an overreaction.

We're driving along when I see my escape. On a lawn near the shoulder of the road: an ancient-looking car with a "$400" sign on it.

"Right here," I say. "Turn right, into the driveway. That's my house."

The house I am referring to resembles an oversized shed. The cab slows down but doesn't stop.

"You passed it."

He doesn't respond.

"You passed it," I say louder.

"Look, son, sit tight, all right? All right? I don't want no trouble but look, I heard all 'bout it on the radio and I'm going to take you to the police station and we'll sort everything out there."

"You can't," I say.

"Sorry, man."

"No. I mean, you can't. What you didn't hear on the radio is I have a gun." I jam my hand against his headrest, like I'm holding something to it. "Stop the car. Now."

"You don't have a gun, son, I know you don't have a gun," he says. His voice is higher than normal though.

"You want to bet your life on it?"

# 4

## Flight to Troy (Population, 23)

Hermes, god of cunning, wit, athletics, commerce, traveling, and in this modern age, *traffic*, intervenes. The cars in front of us brake for a red light. The cabbie yells something at me—*I don't hear.* My belt is unbuckled and I'm dragging Socrates and my stuff out and into the street. The car behind the cab brakes, tires squeal. Beeping. Everyone's beeping. Lanes of cars blocking me in. A red SUV with the window down, a teenage girl staring open-mouthed. I give the cab a backward glance—a part of me wants to say something, maybe wish the cabbie luck, tell him not to blame the little one for sucking the ma's tit dry. The rest of me slaps that part upside the head, tells it not to be a sentimental idiot, and forces my body into motion. I dodge through the cars and into the woods at the edge of the road.

It takes me a while to find my way back to the shed. I knock on the door. A thin, graying man with yellowed nails opens it halfway. "I don't care what you're selling, I'm not interested. Not one more petition. Or a Bible. And I have more than enough boxes of Exotic Nepalese Tea."

"But I'm interested. In your car, I mean. Is it—err, in working condition?"

The man smiles at me like I told him I think his hair is pretty.

"Runs like a bird. A migratory bird," he tells me. "Even comes with a complimentary tank o' gas," he adds, like this is a *major* selling point.

"Great. Great. Also, you wouldn't have a baby seat, would you?"

He hesitates, but only for a moment. "I think I can find you something, for an extra—hundred."

"But you're selling the car for four hundred."

"And I'm selling the baby seat for a hundred. You want it or not?"

Five hundred dollars later, and we're in. Socrates is in

the back, fastened awkwardly into a baby seat that looks old enough to have predated the first automobile. I stick the key into the ignition, turn, and nothing, nothing, nothing.

I get out of the car and knock on the man's door. Again. He is not quite as happy to see me the second time.

"No return policy," he says, and begins to shut the door. "Feel free to migrate your way out of here. Just follow the birds."

"Right, I'm on it, but—*just*—how do you start the car?"

The door opens back up, just long enough for him to sneer at me and say, "Hold down the clutch. Put in the key. Turn. Let go of the clutch."

I finally manage to get the car started—we're rolling, rolling down the slope of the yard, into the shoulder, and onto the road. Relief sweeps over me, but then, I try to shift into first, can't, so we're left moving at a steady three-and-a-half miles per hour. A honking car whizzes by, then another.

*The clutch.* The damn clutch.

I press down on it with my left foot and shift into first gear. I stall. More cars whizz past, honking. I honk at them. My heart hammers so hard it hurts. I wipe the sweat off my face and try again, this time accelerating when I shift into first gear. *It works.* I'm still going a good fifteen miles below the speed limit but the car is in first and that's just about the best feeling in the world.

As if on cue, someone shouts, "Get off the road, asshat!" from a passing car, and my engine begins to emit I'm-going-to-explode sounds. *Oops.* I shift up, and this seems to satisfy it for the time being. I let out a long sigh and drive.


Socrates sleeps and I drive. Over the waters of the Kenduskeag and past the cemetery. Somewhere past the airport I reach a point where I don't recognize anything, but I'm still thinking about the cemetery—the cemetery, and humanity's eventual end.

Yeah, that's fucking right.

It's my birthday, I tried to almost kill myself 'cause of Facebook, I'm driving around with a kidnapped baby named *Socrates*, and all I can think of is whether it'll be nukes that get us, or a supernova, or maybe even the demolition of our planet to make way for a new intergalactic traffic lane.

The suckiest part is that nobody will ever know! Nobody will ever know that we were even here!

"I'm sorry, buddy," I say to Socrates. He's in his basket in the back, all bundled up in the blanket I bought for him. "I mean it's kind of a bummer, isn't it? The death of the human race. Really kind of a drag. But then, it's not like we'll live to see it. Unless our consciousnesses are saved onto a computer or something like that. So why is it so fucking sad?"

He doesn't answer, so I ask again. "Why is it so fucking sad, buddy?"

I try to imagine his response . . . maybe it's the adrenaline, that or just me being crazy, but I get it. I know what he'd say. He'd say, *"You're a romantic, Jack. That's why."*

"Am not," I protest.

*"Correction: a romantic in denial. The first step toward admitting you have a problem is denying it."*

"That doesn't even make sense. The first step toward *not* admitting you have a problem is also *denying it.*"

*"Exactly."*

"But I don't have a problem. I'm not—look, romantics watch romantic comedies. *I* don't believe in fairy-tale love and soul mates and I'm pretty sure if I told a modern-day girl we were meant to be together 'cause she lost her shoe at some dumb dance and I happened to find it, well, she'd probably whip out a can of pepper spray before I had a chance to say 'Someone never saw *Cinderella*.'"

"*So you did watch* Cinderella. *And how did it make you feel?*"

"What are you, my therapist? It made me feel like over-throwing the patriarchy. Prince-in-shining-armor rides in to save the damsel-in-distress yet again—"

"*Overthrowing the patriarchy is not incompatible with romanticism, Jack. There's nothing wrong with being a romantic. Don't be ashamed to say that* Cinderella *made you feel warm inside.*"

"*Everything's* wrong with being a romantic and *Cinderella* did *not* make me feel warm inside. Romantics get hurt, Socrates. The world isn't like what they want it to be, and sooner or later they realize that and get hurt."

"*People get hurt. People who care, and feel. The only way not to get hurt is not to feel, and not to care.*"

"Maybe it's better not to care."

"*Is that really what you believe? Is that what you would wish for your son?*"

I glance at Socrates in the rearview. "No—*no.*"

*"You want him to care. To feel. To be happy. To find true love, whatever that is. Isn't that a kind of romanticism?"*

"No. That's—that's different. Look—whatever. Forget about it. We need to figure out where to go."

*"Fine. Forgetting about it. As long as you don't take me to Athens, I'm good."*

I'm pissed about him calling me a romantic. No, rather, I'm pissed about him *being right.* I let it go though. "Yeah, I don't blame you, but things have changed some since you were there last—for one, to the best of my knowledge, drinking hemlock has gone out of fashion."

*"Pity, there are still a few people I would've liked to see take a swig or two of the stuff."*

"Those people are all long dead," I point out.

*"The deadness of others doesn't seem to deter you, considering whom you're talking to, so why should it deter me?"*

"But I've brought you back. In a way. I've brought you back by naming my son after you, and what have you done to repay me? Lumped me in a category with soppy-eyed couch potatoes watching pretty people live out their pretty little lives on some fancy brand-new fifty-inch plasma screen, oblivious to the fate of our ever-expanding universe."

"*So what is the fate of our ever-expanding universe, Jack?*"

"*. . .*"

"*Jack?*"

"The fate of our ever-expanding universe is ever-expansion. But here's the real question. How am I even communicating with you, anyway? The closest I got to learning Greek was memorizing how to spell *Thermopylae* for 'World in Antiquity.'"

No answer.

Now that I've dispelled the illusion of him, I can't bring him back.

I turn on the radio halfheartedly—it is a poor substitute for an imaginary conversation with a great philosopher. We make do with what we have though, and I have a man on the radio going on about the indictment in Singapore of the owner of an International Traveling Camel Circus on charges of drug trafficking. "*The question America is forced to reckon with, the moral and ethical dilemma that our great country needs to come to terms with, is whether a foreign court has the right to sentence an American citizen to death. For me, the answer is clear. Only Americans should ever, ever have the right to fry other Americans. To stand by and do nothing here is to set a dire precedent. A precedent of allowing foreign countries to determine the fates of any and all American citizens who dip into the waters of drug-trafficking-via-circus-animal. And this, this I simply cannot abide . . ."*

The radio fades into background noise. The dotted yellow line stretches out into the horizon like one of those infinite-length lines you see in math. If only we spent our time talking about those damn infinite-length lines. Like, take a number line that starts at one and goes on to infinity, like this:

$$x\text{------->}$$
$$1\ 2\ 3\dots\infty$$

and a second number line that starts at two and goes on to infinity, like this:

$$x\text{------->}$$
$$2\ 3\ 4\dots\infty$$

Is the first line bigger than the second? It should be. But it *can't* be, because they're both infinite. You can't add one to something that never ends. Or *can* you?

"It just doesn't make sense," I say, to Socrates, *my* Socrates. "Infinity doesn't make *any* sense. We should be talking about *infinity*, not camels. Or if we must talk about camels, it should only be in regard to their relationship to infinity!"

Socrates says nothing, just scrunches up his little face in his sleep.

We pass signs for food, signs for bathrooms, signs for no bathrooms, and even signs for upcoming signs. A coffin on wheels—sorry, a Mini-Cooper—doing what must be ninety flashes by, leaving a trail of very loud and very bad pop music in its wake. An exit's coming up. For Troy, of all places. Old Socrates said he didn't want to go to Athens, but he never mentioned anything about Troy.

Troy does not meet my expectations. Even calling it a town is an exaggeration. The streets are narrow and the land flat, with wide expanses of forest occasionally giving way to farmland. Houses stick out, here and there, like zits on the face of earth. The place feels eerie, almost deserted, and has this sort of faded quality to it, like old clothes bleached too many times. It reminds me of home, though even Skowhegan is a metropolis compared to Troy.

I don't want to think about home. I want to think about Troy. Not *this* Troy, no, what I want is the *real* Troy.

Socrates is awake, so I pull over, near a block of cement that's trying to pass for a school, to tell him the story of Troy. A boy should grow up believing in myth. Not some patronizing, pedantic fluff about the value of hard work to a pig's mortal well-being, not some nursery school fantasy about a girl with a penchant for losing shoes and finding princes. I'm talking real myths, real heroes, real stories, the sort that an entire civilization, not just its youngest members, believed in. The story of Troy goes like this: Guy meets girl, guy falls for girl, guy takes girl home to meet Mom and Pops and, oh snap, girl's (ex?)-husband shows up with an army determined to raze guy's city, kill all the men in guy's city, and turn the women and children of guy's city into slaves. I begin with Paris's visit to Sparta.

Socrates starts crying.

*Maybe he doesn't like the story . . .* A stupid thought. I push it away.

I bring him up to the front seat and sit with him propped against my shoulder. I whisper sentimental nonsense into his ear as I rock him: "There's a good boy," and "Come on buddy, it's all right," and "Who's my brave little kidnappee?" But brave little kidnappee keeps screaming his brave little head off. I brace myself before bringing my nose, slowly, ever so slowly, to his bum—and breathe a long, beautiful sigh of relief. I check his makeshift diaper to be sure. Clean.

I fill his bottle with formula and try feeding him, and there it is—the blessed sound of silence. How much to give him? The bottle itself is almost his size. If I let him drink the whole thing he may very possibly pop, and letting your baby pop on his first day in the world, I'm sure, would land me in the Worst Fathers Ever Hall of Fame, right behind Cronus, who ate all his children.

"What you have to understand, Socrates, is that the story of Troy isn't really a story of war, or the gods, or whatever else they teach you in school. It's a story about love. Blind, idiotic love that gets a lot of people killed. But love. And I know what you're thinking. You're thinking 'Well, Da—'"

I stop myself. Almost said "Dad." But that feels wrong. When I am caught, when I am inevitably chased down by the coppers and dragged unceremoniously out of my car, there will be no more of this "Dad" business. Socrates will grow up never even knowing I existed. He might hear about me eventually, if he's curious, and if his adopted parents feel up to honesty, which, given what I'm probably putting them through, they might not be. He might someday track me down on his own, provided I wasn't murdered by Jess (a distinct possibility, at this point). Maybe even arrange a dinner for all of us—me, him, Jess, his parents.

That would be terrible.

*Hey, remember me? Yeah, yeah, I believe we met a while ago, that time I stole your kid who was really my kid. Oh, thanks for asking, things have been swell, just swell, it really wasn't so bad at all, I made some very close friends, very close, sometimes I think we might've gotten too close, ha ha, but you know what they say, nothing brings guys together like a prison shower. Even had two big ol' fellas named Bubba fight over me one time, kinda nice, you know, like a romantic comedy, but in jail and with a few knife fights thrown in. Everyone called me Rapunzel and would say "Rapunzel, let down your pants!" Ah, look at me, yapping like a yap-yapper. Enough about me, how have YOU been?*

Back to Troy. Maybe if I keep talking about Troy, I won't have to think about anything else. "It's—it's a story about love. And I know what you're thinking: Well—well, Jack, what *is* this thing called love? Well, Socrates, I wish I could demystify it for you in a few words, just like that, tell you it is a force created by all living things, surrounding us, penetrating us, and binding the galaxy together. That it's in your cells. Literally. Like, you have these microscopic hippy-love critters swimming around in your cells, connecting you to love, or some pseudobiological rationalization of metaphysical nonsense like that. But the truth is, there are different kinds of love and different kinds of loving and nobody really understands any of them well enough to put it all into anything other than gibberish with a tendency toward sentimentality."

I take a deep breath. He's stopped drinking so I pat his back lightly to make him burp. Think I saw this on some sitcom about pregnant teenagers. He lets out a couple little "blechs."

I begin again, tell him of heroes and war, of a city that falls for love, all while eating the last of my over-greased McDonald's fries. But I stop. Look out the window, at the school, the packed parking lot, the flagpole, Stars and Stripes hanging limp in the still air. Buses are already beginning to line up at the front of the lot to take the kids home. The kids aren't ready to go home, though. Not yet. In the fields off to the left is a playground filled with their tiny shapes, on slides and swings and the jungle gym. Inside, they're bent over journals and tests and illicit notes passed in secret behind a teacher's back. But the bell rings, and it's over. The playground is abandoned, lines of children erupt from the school, and the waiting buses swallow them up.

It's while watching those kids, in my metal Methuselah, with my kidnapped son staring at me cross-eyed, that I remember what I've always *hated* about the Greeks.

"The Greeks thought the three most powerful forces, more powerful than Zeus, even, were these three sisters called the Fates, who represented the past, present, and future. A few days after a birth, the Fates visited the child, and right then, before the child even had a chance to talk or walk or anything, they determined his whole destiny. So that in living his life, the child would just be following in the path the Fates set out for him. Which means—it means that we're just pawns, all of us. Pawns moved around by the fates, living and dying as they decide. It means we don't have free will—and if we don't have free will, then why should anything we do *matter?* Why should who we love or what we fight for and what we die for matter? Who cares about Troy if we're all just puppets on strings?"

To my surprise, Socrates objects. *"Do we not all have free will? Do we not all have choices, make decisions? Who held a gun to your head and forced you to kidnap me? Maybe the fates aren't so much deciding our fate as seeing in advance the lives we'll freely choose to live."*

"Of course we make decisions," I say, munching on a

cold fry. My cell phone vibrates in my pocket for about the millionth time since I turned the vibrate back on, and for the millionth time I ignore it. "Look, Socrates, of course we make decisions, but that doesn't mean we could have made *different* decisions. What determines how we act, if not the person who we are in the moment before we act—the moment in which we decide what to do? The question to ask is not 'Do we make decisions?' but 'Do we have control over *who we are* when we make those decisions?' And I really don't think we do. Who I am now is determined by who I was a second ago, what I'm saying now is determined by what I was thinking a second ago, and what I was thinking a second ago is determined by what I was thinking a second before that. And if you keep rolling back the seconds, ultimately— *ultimately,* everything from Tommy going to the army, to my not having a lot of friends, to my miscarried brother, and hell, if you go back far enough, mom playing Bob Dylan for me when I was just three days old; all of that shapes and determines who I am and therefore what I do. Everything that's *shaped* me *determines* what I do. What we do, how we act—it's just a response to how we've been shaped throughout our lives. It's just us responding to momentum. The result of all these causal forces acting on us that we have no control over—that's what The Fates represent. The causal forces."

The school emits a second, final bell, and the buses begin to pull out onto the road, one by one, some turning right, others left. I'm conscious of how it's just me and Socrates, alone, in the front seat, *together.* Alone and together.

"But look, Socrates—what I wanted to say, the reason why I brought it up is: here's why Troy is important. Forget the determinism stuff for a bit. Troy is important because everyone has a Helen, and everyone has a Troy, and everyone has a Trojan Horse. It doesn't matter if your Helen is named Charles and your Troy is a bathroom in a gay dance club and your Trojan Horse is some drunk guy named Sugar hammering on the door because he's about to shit himself. No matter what you do, the story will play out as if it has already been written, because it *has* already been written. You just haven't read the script. That's why three thousand or however many years later there's a Troy in probably every state of America, probably a Troy in every country in the whole goddamn world!"

But my words leave me feeling empty. Where is *my* Troy? Where are the walls behind which I can escape?

My cell phone vibrates. I turn it off. It's hard to get at while sitting but finally I manage. Before I do, I see the message on the screen.

*Missed Call: BOB*

Again. For the second time that day, I call her back. This time, she picks up.

"Hello?" she says.

"Hi. Hi. Bob it's me—"

"Yosik? Yosik, is that you?"

A simple question that crushes me. I almost say, "No, no, Grandma, it's Jack." Then I recall how, when I was little, I complained to her that my parents didn't give me a Russian name like all the characters in the fairy tales she told me, and so for the rest of the summer she called me Yosik.

"Yes, Bob, it's me. How are—how are you feeling?"

"Oh, Yosik. Wonderful. I'm feeling wonderful. How could I not? The happiest of birthdays to you! The very happiest. I didn't forget. I wrote it down. The key to remembering is to write things down. You never write anything down, but you'll see—"

"You remember, Bob?"

A pause. "Yes. Well. Yes and no. But today's a good

day. I'm remembering the important things. The things that need remembering. Your birthday. I wrote it down so I wouldn't forget. I know you thought I'd forget—I just wish I could visit you, but the doctor said I shouldn't drive—"

"You'd kill someone—"

"Yes, I imagine that's what the doctor would say."

"Bob—do you think we have free will?"

She laughs. I haven't heard her laugh in a long time. "Oh, Yosik. Not this again."

"I'm serious—"

"We'll discuss free will when I see you next—when *am* I going to see you? Will you visit this summer? Like you used to? I never used to like the summer, but now it's my favorite season. It reminds me of you."

"Soon," I say. "Now," I whisper, too low for her to hear. "I've got to go, Bob, but I'll visit, I promise."

I hang up. I hang up and *fucking hell, fucking yes,* I know where I'm going! Grandma's dying, but maybe, before she does, I can introduce her to my *son.* It won't make a difference, but so what? So what if it's futile? Futility can go pop some pills and jump out of a goddamn window. If it matters to her and if it matters to me and if in some small way

I can *shape* Socrates before I have to give him up—well, then it'll be worth it. The city will fall, as it always does, the Greeks will descend on us, take Helen (*Sorry, Socrates*) away, as they always do, but the myth, the spirit, that's what Socrates and Grandma can hold on to no matter how far life and death and time carry them from me.

For just a second or two, I'm elated, knowing now, where to go and what I'm doing. This elation is quickly overwhelmed by a practical assessment of my situation. Socrates has diapers and formula and even a blankie, but I haven't got shit. A sandwich would be nice. There's also the question of gas money. Clifford, New York, is not California, but if I run out of gas in the middle of Maine it might as well be.

Ten minutes from Troy, I see a 7-Eleven. I turn into a lot comprised of exactly three and a half faded parking spaces. An old Cadillac straddles two of them. I sit there for maybe ten minutes, watching the empty road, not wanting to disturb Socrates, until the door to the 7-Eleven opens and a middle-aged Japanese man says something I don't catch.

I roll down my side window and say, "What?"

He says it again, gesticulating at my car, something

about customers, customers, customers—he must mean the parking lot is only for customers. He says something else in Japanese. I don't know Japanese, but I'm guessing he's going on about how this isn't a rest stop for babies and their kidnappers.

"Okay," I say. "Okay, we're coming. We're customers."

When he hears this the man is all smiles. He ushers me inside, where I load up on as many ready-made sandwiches as I can get my hands on. If only they had a cooler. Also: *diapers*. Did I buy enough diapers to get us to Clifford? What is the rate at which babies go through diapers? Does 7-11 even sell diapers? Who knows? Breathe, Jack. Breathe. I whip out my phone, mostly out of habit. There's a new text from Jess.

She says, *Please. Please talk to me. I just want to talk.*

I'm a sucker for the word "please." If you asked me to please rob the bank with you and I liked you even a teeny bit, there's a good chance that within the hour I would be wearing a ski mask, waving a semiautomatic about, yelling at some poor manager to unlock the safe, and generally being a bad guy in a B action movie featuring a heroic hostage-negotiating police officer played by Denzel Washington. All for the word "please." And because I like you a teeny bit. And because Denzel Washington is a badass.

I stare at my phone menu, the screen with contacts and memos and the date in a neat little corner. I've got this cool artsy-fartsy wallpaper. To talk to Jess, or to *not* talk to Jess. If only I had a flower whose petals I could pluck.

A familiar number flashes across my screen. Not Jess. I click Talk.

"Hey, asshole," Tommy K says.

"Hey—" and I'm about to say what I usually say in response, but my eyes stray to Socrates and I leave the greeting hanging.

"You okay, man?" he says, feigning concern.

"I was before you called."

"Ouch. You talk to all the people who call to say 'Happy Birthday, I'm coming over to give you a present' that way?"

"No, just you. Listen, I'm not actually in my room at the moment."

"Oh, you sly, sick canine."

"Wait—what? Am I sly or am I sick?"

"Whatever you are, you're a dog, man. You're having birthday sex, aren't you?"

I throw another nervous glance at Socrates.

"No, no, not exactly, man; you're a little off base on that one."

"But I'm close, right? I'm close? Is it a birthday orgy? If it is I'm so there."

"I know you are, man, I can always count on you."

"Damn right."

"Listen, I'm not at school right now, but I really appreciate you calling."

The Japanese man says that he's having a buy three, get one half-off sale on the Luvs. Just the Luvs though, Huggies are normal price.

"Thanks," I tell him.

Don't know what I would've done with myself if not for that update on the diaper situation.

"Are you talking to someone else, asshole? I'm calling you to say Happy Birthday and you're talking to someone else."

"Well, what can I say, man? That's what happens when you interrupt an orgy—I'm a little preoccupied right now. You're lucky I took your call at all—would you take my call if you were in my place?"

No hesitation. "Nope."

He has no idea. "See?"

"Wow, man. You're, like, a really good friend."

"Thanks, man. All right, I've got to go but I'll call you later."

"Hey, Jack?"

"Yeah?"

"Happy Birthday, man."

"Thanks, man."

Back in the parking lot, the car is dead. I try again, and the engine makes this coughing noise, like an old guy who's smoked his whole life and is about to throw up a black lung. I lean against the headrest and think.

*It's stuffy in here without air-conditioning.* That's the best I can do. Then I call Tommy K back. First thing out of my mouth is, "Wanna come join the fun?"

I neglect to mention the issue of kidnapping.

A half hour later, I'm sitting shotgun in Tommy K's old Ford F150 truck with the windows down, and he's saying, "Okay, man. Let me see if I got all this straight, because, you know, it's a lot to keep track of. You want me to drive you to my house. You want to hide out at my house until it's nighttime. Then you want me to drive you to some hospital I've never heard of so you can pick up the 'it's-complicated' mother of your son, whom, incidentally, you haven't spoken to since you kidnapped her baby, and then you want me to drive you to your half-loony grandma's house while evading the police, FBI, CIA, NSA, SWAT, and Russian secret agents, after which, you plan to turn yourself in, because the whole getaway to Mexico thing is overdone and cliché and you're too good for that shit. Have I missed anything?"

"Nah, man, you've pretty much got it covered. Except—"

"Except? There's *more?*"

"If I could borrow a cooler—it's just that the baby formula will spoil otherwise . . ."

He lets out a long whistle. "Oh, of course. A cooler. For the baby formula. Of course. Why didn't I think of that?" Then, "Insane. In-fucking-sane."

Like that's news to me. My head starts a-spinning whenever I try to understand myself. It's just, *I'm a father now* and I want to do this one thing for my son, to shape him in some tiny way before I have to let him go. Socrates, incidentally, has woken up and started crying again.

"I'm going to get fucking court-martialed for this," he yells over Socrates.

"You're off duty."

"They'll throw me in jail."

"And you'll be thanking me when you're not in a desert getting shot at by a guy who thinks there'll be an extra virgin waiting for him in heaven for every bullet he puts in your ass."

I wait for a witty retort, but none comes, and I grow more and more ashamed at my douche-bag-ness. His enlistment was sudden; he didn't so much talk to me about it as tell me after the fact—it's still somewhat of a sore topic. The army means a lot to him though, and he's risking it for me . . .

"I'm sorry, man. You're helping me and I'm—"

"Never said I was helping," he says, but his heart's not in that threat. Socrates is still crying so we pull over and I stumble to the back. I offer Socrates the bottle but he isn't having it. I check his diaper. *Fuck.* Didn't I just do this at the McDonald's?

"I'm going to need to change him," I say, more to myself than to Tommy. I'm stalling.

"You're *what?*"

"I think it's a big one."

"Damn it, Jack," he says, and rolls the windows down. "Just don't get it on the seats, will you? Not the seats, Jack."

I open the diaper and—my God.

"Tommy?" I gasp.

"Yeah?" he says, craning his head to see.

"You're a great friend, you know that?"

"Oh hell no, Jack. No, no, no, no, no, no."

"*Please?*" I give him the puppy eyes.

He resists for a few seconds, sighs, then scrambles out of the driver's seat without a word. We change him together. Bonding experience is one way to describe it. Tommy crumples Socrates's dirty makeshift diaper up in a ball and pitches it out the window. I give my friend a disapproving look. He says, "Shit is biodegradable, Jack." We clean our hands with Huggies baby-butt wipes.

"Do you love her? The girl? Jess?"

"I don't know," I say. "I thought I did. But I was afraid to tell her. And then she threw a chair at me. *Two*, actually. And now I'm not sure anymore."

He snorts, says something that sounds like "in-fuck-ing-sane" under his breath.

I want him to understand, want to understand myself, so as Tommy revs the engine, I tell him, "Look, I liked Jess a lot, but I always felt like, I don't know, she was only interested in me because all her friends were gone for the summer. We spent most of it together. But then all her college friends came back for the fall and I hardly saw her. I called her less and she called me less and then one day she called and gave me a lecture on frog reproduction and told me she was pregnant."

"Frog reproduction?"

"Frog reproduction," I say. "Don't ask." I pause. "I do think maybe I love him, though."

"Him?"

"Socrates."

"Socrates," he repeats, eyes wide. "Oh my god. You really are crazy, aren't you? Like, not even ha-ha-my-best-friend's-a-little-wack crazy, but like, full-on-sixth-effing-sense crazy. That orgy we were talking about before. . . Were you having it with a bunch of dead philosophers? Is that what this is all about? You fell in love with Socrates while sucking the old guy off or something?" His voice is oddly flat and I can't tell if he's joking or not.

"Socrates is my son," I say.

"Oh! Of course," he says, and laughs nervously. "So you adopted some old Greek post-mortem and kidnapped a baby for good measure. All in one day. Christ, Jack, I had no idea you were so set on starting a family."

"Tommy. Socrates *is* my son."

Then he gets it. He lets out a long, long sigh. "Shit, man. You had me scared. You had me scared. I thought . . . I didn't know what to think. I thought you'd completely lost it."

"I named the little guy for some dead Greek I fell in love with after sucking him off at an imaginary orgy."

He punches me in the shoulder. I punch him back and he's all, like, "DRIVING MAN," and it's good to see Tommy K again. It's like old times, when we went to the same school and he wasn't going to goddamn Afghanistan. Aside from the few persistent bits of baby shit still under our fingernails, that is.

"Hey, Jack?"

"Yeah?"

"Now that we got the little stuff out of the way, I've got something really important for you."

"Yeah?"

"Open the glove compartment."

I look from the handle of the glove compartment to Tommy and back with suspicion.

"Go on."

I do.

Inside, I find *Pokémon: The First Movie—Mewtwo vs. Mew.*

"Happy Birthday."

"You—*son of a bitch.*"

"I knew you'd like it. It even comes with a collectible, holographic promo card."

"You son of a bitch."

"What? You told me it was your favorite movie."

"Sure it was. When I was like, eight."

"Don't lie."

"Ten."

"Don't lie."

"Okay, so I might've watched it again when I was thirteen."

"Better."

"And fourteen. And fifteen. Oh, fuck it, Tommy, it's what I've always wanted."

"I know, man, I know."

"It's like I got up today and I thought, man,

wouldn't it be great if someone gave me *Pokémon: The First Movie—Mewtwo vs. Mew* for my birthday present. And here it is."

"There it is, Jacky-boy, waiting for you. Take her in. Breathe her in. Caress her. I'll pretend to concentrate on driving." He winks at me.

"Gee, thanks, man."

But I resist the temptation. Best to leave the holding, caressing, and breathing in of *Pokémon: The First Movie—Mewtwo vs. Mew* for a more private time. I do have a few free moments by myself, just me and the movie, when Tommy stops at a bank on Main Street back in Bangor to withdraw some money, but I text Jess instead.

*Hey. I kno ur prbly rly worried but were fine.*

A few minutes pass before she answers. *Cant believe u. U didn't even want the goddamn kid and*

I wait for the second part of her text. It doesn't come. Maybe she doesn't know what comes after the "and."

*I dnt kno. just felt like, I needed 2 say bye. not gonna keep him I just want 2 say bye.*

*Hes a day old Jack.*

*He might nt remember but I will. Maybe he will2, somewhere deep down. I got 2 do this Jess.*

*U named him Socrates?*

*Figured it out huh?*

*Yea. Ur crazy, u kno that.*

I wonder if her not posing the last bit as a question is intentional or not.

*Ppl keep tellin me.*

*Dont know if Im even mad at u anymore, which makes me think Im goin crazy. Im just rly, rly tired. And buzzd from pain-killers. Tired and buzzd.*

*sry*

*Kidnappings not the kind of thing sry will get u out of drling.*

I feel a nostalgic pang in my chest.

All those parties we went to . . . I hated the loud, obnoxious music and the smell of sweat mixed with weed mixed with alcohol, I hated how you couldn't move without bumping into someone, without getting pushed or smooshed or groped. But I loved how we used to call each other darling and trade meaningful looks about this drunk or that drunk without even saying a word.

*We're sitting on Michael Bentler's back lawn, which is rather unstable, as far as back lawns go. Or maybe this is the true state of back lawns, and we only ever see them as they really* are after two rounds of beer pong and four shots of vodka. Who knows, really?

"What can we know for sure if we don't even really understand Time?" I ask aloud, to Jess, then somehow segue into a semi-incoherent monologue on Nietzsche's Eternal Return. Semi-incoherent because I'm not even sure I completely understand it when I'm sober: "If time is infinite and there are only a finite number of ways for matter to be arranged, then everything that's happened has to happen again and again and on into infinity, right? According to statistics, I mean? Now if you take infinite return and combine it with Laplace's Demon—"

She pretends to watch two drunk guys wrestling in the pool. I poke her. And again.

People employing the silent treatment always have less patience than the ones they're trying to silence. Finally she groans and asks me, "Jack, why must you always be obsessed with philosophy when you're drunk?"

I take offense. "I'm not obsessed, and anyway, if you're not interested in talking about the eternal recurring inevitability of us sitting here right now, which is pretty fucking amazing if you ask me, then I guess we can just talk about other things, like what you're going to do with a major in

*communications when you graduate and—are you even listening
to me?"*

*Her eyes have turned back to the wrestling match in the pool,
which is looking less and less like wrestling and more and more
like rough—*

*"Sorry," she says. "I can't help it. The one doing the head-
locking is kind of hot, wouldn't you say?"*

*"Nah, I prefer the other one."*

*"The one turning blue?"*

*"I think that's the light. Anyway, underdogs are hot. Plus
look at those pecs."*

*She pinches me.*

*"Ow! Jealous much?"*

*"No. I just don't like to see you objectifying him. He's not a
sex object, you know."*

*"That's what he thinks."*

*She pinches me again.*

*"Ow!"*

*"That time I was jealous."*

*Somewhat clumsily, I bring my lips to hers, and we kiss.*

I type out a text and stare at it for a few seconds.

*I want u2 com with us. So u can say bye 2. He's ur son 2.*

I wince, and click SEND.

*How u goin 2 say gdbye? Word not good enough 4 u?*

Here it comes. I text her, *I want to take him to see my grandma.*

I don't bother trying to explain. About her Alzheimer's and her calling today, my promise to her, and how maybe if I bring her and him together, I don't know, it'll give them both something meaningful, because I know it doesn't make sense, none at all. It sounds like some New Age bullshit, but there it is. I know it'll mean something. I know it will matter. I know it feels right, I know I owe it to him, but I can't just say all that to her. No, literally, I can't. My phone limits the size of texts to eighty characters. Eighty characters just doesn't cut it for this.

*ur grandma*

Again, no question mark.

*Yep*

*i dont understand*

So I put on my rather loose-fitting Jack-the-messiah hat and text her, still with my impeccable grammar in place, *Trust me. Will you do that? One more time?*

She doesn't respond. She might go and tell the cops. Somehow though, I don't think she will. She didn't really get to say good-bye to him, either.

*Will you still be in the hospital tonight?*

Tommy's back in the car, complaining about how old ladies don't know how to use ATMs, that they're always swiping their cards the wrong way, when I get an answer from Jess.

*Yea.*

# 5

## Siren Who's Not Looking for the Nearest Dunkin' Donuts

Tommy's old truck looks way out of place in the driveway of his mini-mansion of a house, complete with two hyper-pretentious Greek columns on either side of the front door. His parents apparently gave him a new BMW for his seventeenth birthday. He told me he sold it, bought this piece-of-crap truck, and blew the rest of the money on stocks, investing in some Argentinian company that went belly-up, but the stocks game seems much more his parents' game than his, and Tommy always tries to be as little like his parents as possible. Sometimes I think he enlisted just to spite them, but that's not the kind of thing you accuse your best friend of.

"Home sweet home," he says.

Tommy shepherds us quickly up to his room, like he's afraid I might not make it. There are pictures of him everywhere, on the walls, lining dressers. Tommy K's a good-looking kid but a lot of the photos aren't even that great. I spot the one that Tommy always refers to as his serial killer mug and I have to laugh.

In his room, Tommy falls backward onto his queen-size bed with a sigh. I set Socrates's basket down near the bed, and the little guy stares past me, up at the ceiling, with those wide eyes of his. When I don't move, he throws me a questioning look: *"Hey, man, you're blocking the view."*

And I'm, like, *"It's a ceiling, man. Get over yourself."*

And he's, like, *"No, man, you don't get it. There's a ceiling on the house, but what about when we're outside? Does* outside *have a ceiling? Where does* outside *end?"*

And I'm, like, *"The sky's the ceiling outside,"* but even as I say that, I know what he's getting at. You keep going and the sky turns to space and where is the ceiling of space? Does it simply keep going and going, with no ceiling at all? How is that possible, for something to keep going forever like that? Especially because it did have a ceiling once, fifteen billion years ago. The distance between the floor and the ceiling of the universe was less than an inch, back then. And now, fifteen billion years later, there's no ceiling anymore? How does that work? And if there *is* a ceiling, then what is outside the ceiling of the universe? Is there an infinite regress of ceilings, or simply no ceiling at all?

Socrates answers my rhetorical question by bringing up Plato's cave. *"We're chained up and we can't get out. Just like we'll never break free of our chains, we'll never know the truth about ceilings, whether something lies beyond the last ceiling, or if there is even such a thing as a last ceiling. But I think you need to* believe *in a last ceiling, a ceiling to end all ceilings, a ceiling that* limits *the unlimited, and renders the universe comprehensible. You can't reach the world outside the cave, but you have to believe in it, believe it's out there."*

"*But,*" I tell him, "*You're just evading a question you don't have an answer for. You're trading knowledge for belief.*"

"*I'm trading knowledge of the universe for knowledge of us,*" Socrates says. "*Just like we have to believe the sun will come up tomorrow, even though we don't* know *it will, we also have to find a way of making sense of the universe.*

*And infinity—the infinite regress—is the opposite of making sense, isn't it? We have to limit the universe somehow. It's like what you said in Troy—I'm not talking about a* literal *ceiling. I'm talking about* your *ceiling. How do* you *limit the universe? How do* you *make sense of infinity when* your *Greeks are at the gates of* your *Troy?*

"Hey," Tommy says. "You and Sir Craps-a-Lot having a staring contest over there or something?"

I smile in spite of myself. "That's my son you're talking about, dickwad."

"You know what they say, the apple doesn't fall far from the tree."

"What if the apple tree is on the top of Mount Everest?"

"Then it would be a dead apple tree and there wouldn't be any apples. You know how cold it is up there?"

"No."

"Me neither, but that doesn't stop me from speculating about things I have no clue about."

"My point is just that sometimes apples do fall far from the tree and I resent the implication that I crap my pants."

"And my point is simply that Sir Craps-a-Lot has to get it from somewhere."

On the floor, to my right, there's an inside-out Ralph Lauren sock. I didn't even know Ralph made socks. I pick it up, turn it into a sock ball.

"Don't do it," he says.

I do it.

"Jerk."

It feels weird to act the way I always do with Tommy now that I'm a father. How can you be both a father and a friend at once?

"So, Jack," he says. "You do like your birthday present, right?"

"'Course man."

"So you'd really like to watch it, right?"

"Obviously."

"Now, right?" He nods to his plasma screen, and the VHS/DVD player on the floor beneath it.

"Oh, there's nothing I'd love more but I'm afraid I forgot it in the car."

"I didn't," Tommy says, and raises the box triumphantly in the air. *Bastard.*

"Well, in that case," I say.

And so we watch Pokémon in silence. It's almost like a staring contest. We're both waiting for the other to blink. I blink first, by suggesting we play a game while *obviously* continuing to watch the movie.

"Monopoly?" I say.

"Workers of the world, unite," he says. "You have nothing to lose but your chains!"

"I take that as a no?"

"Intuitive as always, Jacky-boy."

"Chess?"

"Requires too much brainpower."

"Checkers?"

"I want to go on the record as being very much against games that make a game of war."

We settle on Risk. I'm invading Asia right around the time the movie ends with this epic showdown between Mew and Mewtwo. The movie wasn't actually as bad as I was hyping it up to be. Kind of a Pokémon version of *Frankenstein*, and *Frankenstein* was just a modern take on Prometheus, who stole fire from Zeus and gave it to man. Both *Pokémon: The First Movie—Mewtwo vs. Mew* and *Frankenstein* suggest that playing with (Zeus's) fire will lead to a second-degree burn. Prometheus suggests it'll lead to you getting your liver plucked out of you over and over again for all eternity. We continue our game of world domination until I have to stop to feed Socrates.

"Putting off the inevitable under the guise of being a semi-responsible father slash babynapper, eh, Jack?" Tommy says as I pick up Socrates's bottle off the floor. I head for the kitchen, where we stuck the formula, pausing at the doorway to say, "More like taking pity and giving you a few more minutes to breathe."

With this, I work my right shoe off, and scream in my best Russian accent, "We will bury you!"(I'm playing as Red).

Tommy laughs. "Dude, all you have is Australia."

"And don't you forget it."

I return with a full bottle, and Tommy watches me, real quiet, while I let Socrates drink his fill.

"Where are your parents, anyway?" I ask.

"Working." He doesn't elaborate. For a while the only sound comes from Socrates's thirsty gulping.

I don't say anything. Sometimes nothing's the right thing to say.

"What does it feel like, Jack," he asks, any semblance of kidding gone. "What's it like to be a dad?"

I give him a tired smile, and say, "Honestly, Tommy? I'm still figuring it out."

"Ha."

"Ha."

Tommy lies on the floor, arms crossed behind his back. "Well, he's still breathing, so you're doing okay in my book. If not for making it onto *America's Most Wanted*, I might even give you a C-plus."

"Thanks, mate."

"Taking the whole I-own-Australia bit to heart, I see."

Then I say, "You know, I told her I thought she should have an abortion."

"Oh."

"Yeah."

He goes quiet. "It's scary. Must be scary."

I hold Socrates as he drains the contents of the bottle down, down, down. It's crazy, really crazy, but when you think about it, my moment of drunken ecstasy with Jess changed the whole fucking world, the whole goddamn universe, because now my son is here, he *exists*. It's like throwing a pebble in a pond. The pond's rippling waters will evaporate and rain down in a thousand places all over the earth. They will fall into the mouths of children. They will fall into puddles and lakes and rivers and oceans. They will set the whole world a-rippling. Maybe this is what Socrates was talking about—*limiting* the universe by *changing* it.

It's not scary. Scary doesn't cover it. It's terrifying. Should some seventeen-year-old me have the power to shape all of existence by being too dumb to put a rubber on right? Just this morning I was . . . and now, now I want more than anything to stick around. To see all the little ways Socrates will go about making the universe *his* own . . .

"You okay there, man?" Tommy asks.

"Yeah," I say. The bottle's empty. Burping time. Socrates lets a couple rip from the wrong end, but whatever.

"Wanna finish?" Tommy nods to the board. I look at the vast horde of blue, then at my own red comrades holding strong in Australia, and say, "For ze motherland!"

"I'll take that as a yes."

The doorbell rings at a quarter to ten. I exchange a glance with Tommy, who shrugs. "I'll see who it is. You stay here," he says, as if preempting a habit of mine to greet strangers from the doorways of friends' homes.

He thumps down the stairs and I go over to the

window to look. Fear wells up cold inside me—a police cruiser is parked at the end of Tommy's long driveway, lights flashing.

I'm breathing hard. I can feel my heartbeat in my ears. That *can't* be healthy.

Finally I hear the front door close. The policeman walks back to his car and drives off.

"We should move," Tommy says, striding into his room. "That was the police."

"I know."

"They're looking for you."

"And here I was thinking he was asking for directions to the nearest Dunkin' Donuts."

Tommy humors me with a thin smile.

"Tommy," I say, suddenly coming to a decision. "I've changed my mind."

His eyebrows arch up.

"I can't involve you in this. Socrates isn't your son. It's not fair to bring you into this. I can get him to my grandma's house. I'll figure it out. My car's at the hospital. It's not fair for me to—"

"Shut up, man," he says, and rolls his eyes. "You want to know why I joined the army?"

I want to point out that this might not be the best time to have this conversation, but I make a conscious decision to be a dick instead.

"Girls like a guy in uniform? Guys like a guy in uniform? Hell, *I* like a guy in uniform. Everyone does. I get it."

"Shut up, man," he says. "I joined because life is so fucking boring. From five to eighteen we get up at six-thirty, go to school by eight, get home round three-thirty—"

"You're exaggerating. I'm pretty sure the schedule changes a bit when you jump from elementary to middle and from middle to high—"

"Shut up, man. Where was I?"

"Existential angst about the pointlessness of our mundane existences, case in point, the immutability of school schedules."

"Right," he says. "And then you get home and maybe run around with your friends for a few hours and watch some TV and do your homework and then you go to bed and repeat, and repeat. They expect us to do the same thing for four more years, and maybe two to four after that, if we want a real good job like a lawyer or a doctor, and once we get our fancy pieces of paper we do the whole school routine all over again, except now it's called a *job* and we're not even learning anymore, just going through the motions of yesterday."

"You're such a poet, Tommy. Seriously. You're making me swoon."

"*Shut up,* man. And then we have kids and we watch them go through exactly what we went through and it's all so quiet and boring and circular. I want a fucking explosion, man. Girls go to the movies to get hot for the guys they'll never get and guys go to the movies to see shit they'll never blow up get blown up."

He looks at me expectantly, like that's my cue to pop someone in the head or something, but all I can think of is how it's true what they say. Insanity is a disease, and it is highly contagious.

"Man," I say, "you're my best friend, and I know it's socially unacceptable for me to admit this, but I love you, in a strictly platonic sort of way, I'm pretty sure, I'm kinda sure, I'm unsure, anyway, point being, two crazies and a baby is a recipe for disaster."

"Then let's make it three crazies."

I stare at him. "You're just gonna leave me hanging on the love bit?"

He shrugs at me sheepishly, then says, "That was the plan." Then, quieter, with his eyes averted, he says, "I love you, too, man." And then louder, "But if you try to kiss me or something I will choke you."

"That's kind of hot. Will you do it in uniform?"

# 6

## The Yellow Brick Road to the Hospital

The Yellow Brick Road to the Hospital

The screen of Tommy's GPS lights up the inside of his truck.

"Put in the address, will you?" Tommy says, turning the key. The engine grumbles to life just as I finish buckling Socrates into his car seat.

"Sure," I say, but quickly encounter some difficulties. "Umm—Tommy?"

"Yeah?" he says distractedly, as he backs out of his driveway.

"Is this thing in—*German*?"

"That it is, Jacky-boy."

"Tommy, you don't *speak* German."

"*Granate! Deckung nehmen!*"

"Well, I take it back. You could move to Germany right this second if you wanted."

*Granate! Deckung nehmen!* translates to "grenade take cover." We both know it from *Medal of Honor*, this game we used to play online when online shooters were actually good.

"Well, maybe not right this *very* second, but yeah, I think I'd be able to get by."

With a bit of guidance from Tommy, I do eventually manage to input the hospital's address. It takes a few seconds to load, after which a yellow line appears, stretching out from the blue dot representing our car past the edge of the screen.

"Just like Alice," he says.

"Dorothy," I correct.

"Dorothy. Whatever. Dumb story, anyway."

We follow this yellow brick road of ours, and fifteen minutes later, we're in the parking lot, right by St. Patrick's. The GPS system triumphantly declares, *"Wir haben eingetroffen!"*

"Now what?" Tommy asks.

"Now we wait and see if crazy number three will show up," I say.

I text her, *We're here. Come out.* We wait in the darkness, engine off, with the moon bright and high, until my phone explodes into vibrations.

"Shit," Tommy says under his breath.

*Where r u Jack?*

I read the message aloud.

"Could be a trap," he says, and even in the dark, I know we're both thinking of the same thing, Admiral Fish-Face in *Revenge of the Jedi* going, "IT'S A TRAP."

"You're such a nerd," I say, and punch him in the shoulder.

"What?" he says, genuine surprise in his voice. Maybe I overestimated his geekiness.

"Just flash your lights. If it's a trap it's a trap."

"You don't say," he says, but obliges.

Several things happen in rapid succession. Jess limp-runs into view, wearing one of those hospital gowns that you think is a joke until the doctor tells you to put it on. At the far end of the parking lot, lights flare. They flash red, white, and blue. I *knew* they'd have someone waiting at the hospital. I could be fucking Jason Bourne with a little practice. Emphasis on the *be*, not the *fucking*.

Jess reaches the truck and pulls frantically on the

locked door. I fumble to open it. Then she's in, huffing, finding her way into the cramped back to where Socrates is, only now the police car is rolling toward us, signaling with its lights for us to stay where we are. We do no such thing. Tommy puts his foot to the gas and we pull a U-turn before spilling out of the parking lot and into the night.

"I believe introductions are in order," I say in a rather high voice. "Jess, this is Tommy; Tommy, Jess."

Jess does not speak, she's still catching her breath. Running from cops is probably on her list of things to refrain from doing for a while. My orthodontist gave me a list when I got my braces and it said no gum for three years and WHY AM I THINKING ABOUT MY BRACES NOW?

"You're the girl who threw a chair at Jack, right?" Tommy asks. "He told me all about you."

"Two," I say. "It was two chairs. Not one after another—there was time in between—"

"What am I doing here?" Jess asks.

I turn around in my seat, meaning to tell her something reassuring. Before I can, Tommy says, "Shit," and hits the accelerator. I see the police car in the rearview.

The GPS shouts, "*Umdrehen sofort!*"

The arrow on the speedometer goes up and up, forty, fifty, sixty, but the siren keeps following, calling to us, it wants to lead us astray.

"Slow down," Jess says.

"*Umdrehen sofort!*"

"Turn on the goddamn radio," Tommy says.

"Slow down," Jess says, louder.

"*Umdrehen sofort!*"

We take a turn, fast, and another, and we're going seventy on a straightaway—just us and the blazing siren beating back the darkness.

Tommy: "Jack, *THE RADIO*—"

Jess: "YOU'RE GOING TO KILL US."

GPS: "*Umdrehen sofort!*"

I'm trying to turn on the radio, really, I am, but I can't find it, can't find the button. All of a sudden, click—our cabin fills with Kansas's "Dust in the Wind." Tommy lowers the windows, and that's how we race through the night.

Minutes later, Tommy motions for me to cut the music. He waits until we put a turn between the cop and us, then coasts us into some driveway and turns the engine off.

"*Links abbiegen auf Victor Spur, dann gehen sie zwei meilen!*"

We wait. Wait. And the police cruiser rushes past. We stay like that for some time, in silence. Then, to my right, the door clicks open. Jess scrambles out of the truck with Socrates in her arms. Screw sirens, she's hollering like a banshee. Tommy and I run after her, tripping over wet earth, rocks, broken branches. She's headed for the house, gets as far as this tiny playground. In the light of the moon the red kiddy slide, tire swing, and sand pit look lonely and timeless, like nobody has ever played here, will ever play here. Near the slide Jess's foot catches on something. She slips and almost drops Socrates, who's crying now. We reach her as she's getting up. She looks at me like I'm some kind of monster.

"This has to stop, Jack. This has to stop," she says.

We meet each other's eyes.

*"Keep them open this time."*

*"They want to close, Jess. They like closing. It's like when you sneeze, your eyes close, you know? They just go and do it. It's a reflex."*

*"You're comparing kissing me to* sneezing?*"*

*"Darling, when you say it like that it sounds bad."*

*"It* is *bad, dear. I'm not quite sure what to say right now."*

*"Come, on Jess—" I lean in but she pushes me away.*

"*I know you're new at this, Jack, but making a girl feel like she gives you an allergic reaction—*"

"*Not you. Just your kisses.*"

"*—before you've even had sex? Not a smart move, Jack. You pretty much just killed your chances—*"

"*Darling—*"

"*Torpedoed them. Nuked them. Anti-matter-bombed them.*"

"*What can I do to make it up to you?*" I say, in my best impression of the deep and sexy voice I don't have.

She frowns. "*Promise me you'll keep your eyes open whenever we kiss.*"

"*Done.*"

"*The whole time, Jack. No dozing off halfway through.*"

"*Done. So is sex still out of the—*"

"*Don't push your luck, dear.*"

Jess was right. You see this special flash in someone's eyes when your lips meet theirs. You can't put it into words, but it's there. It's almost like we have this flash now, even though we're not kissing.

She speaks, quieter. "We could have all gotten killed back there, you idiots realize that?" But she's only talking to me. Just me. "It has to stop. You can go to a police station and turn yourself in. We can go together. They'll go easy on you. We don't even have to involve Tommy. Tommy can go home."

"Tommy doesn't want to go home," Tommy says from my side. "Tommy wants to help his crazy-ass friend introduce his grandma to Socrates."

"But why?" Jess asks. There's this shakiness in her voice. "What's going to change? You think you're going to get there and something magical's going to happen? Jack, you do realize that there's a good chance we'll get there and your grandma won't even remember who you are."

"Yeah," I say. "I know. But she called me, Jess. She called me today and I talked to her and she remembered. She remembered my birthday. I gotta try. It'll mean so much to her. And Socrates—"

"His name is not goddamn Socrates."

"Please, Jess."

"Go fuck yourself." She's holding Socrates tight to her breast. He's squirming, crying.

"You're hurting him," I say.

"Fuck you," she says, but loosens her grip on him.

"Jess," I say, dropping to my knees. "I'm sorry. I'm really, really, really sorry. I was just scared. I mean, the idea of us being able to bring *him* into this world, that's what's crazy about all this. That's what's crazy. Everything else, everything else I've done . . ."

If only I could tell her, about the universe, about how Socrates thinks that by changing the universe we limit it. How maybe Socrates is the way she and I have limited it.

The lights go on in the house. I throw Tommy a look that's supposed to convey *oh crap*. He throws me one the little code-breakers in my head decipher as *This is your fault*. The front door swings open, revealing a great mass of a man in tighty-whities much too small for his significant assets. In his hands, a shotgun. He works his way onto a wooden porch, chest hair glinting in the light streaming from the open door.

He frowns at us, and we're all frozen. *Run.* Run. Now is when we run. Just as he opens his mouth to speak a woman's voice hollering from inside cuts him off. "Is it those vandals again? That gun's not loaded, you know! What are you going to do with an unloaded gun? Play cops and robbers? Aren't you a little old for that?"

He throws a glance over his shoulder. "Shut up, Marie, you're not helping."

"Don't you let them take our mailbox again. Herbert?

Are you listening to me? Don't you let them—"

"Marie. Shut up."

"I'll shut you up, you brute. Don't you tell me to shut up or I'll—"

"Marie!" he yells. "Shut up."

You don't get second opportunities to flee like this, life just doesn't give you cues so obvious and blatant. But nobody moves. Nobody moves—I watch as a smile creeps onto Tommy's face. I can't help myself—I'm smiling, too.

The fat man with a shotgun shakes his head and talks, more to himself than to us. "Catch her during the day and she's a regular old Nurse Jekyll, but wake her up in the middle of the night and Nurse Jekyll's stepped out, but Mrs. Hyde's in . . ." He clears his throat and dons a frown once more. "Anyway—"

"Did you just call me *old?*" Mrs. Hyde says through a doorway that all the laws of nature seem to suggest she cannot possibly fit through. In her hands—another shotgun.

"Marie," he says, turning to face her. "What *are* you doing?"

"Herbert, do you have your hearing aid in, because I

swear I just told you not three seconds ago that that shot-gun isn't loaded. This is the one that's loaded," she says, shaking the gun in her hands.

"Marie," he says, with a grunt of frustration, "get back in the house."

But Mrs. Hyde, she squints at us, takes a step forward, and then screams, "Herbert!"

"What?!"

"Those are *kids*. What in god's holy hell are you doing assaulting a bunch of kids in your underwear with an unloaded shotgun?"

"Marie—"

"Is that a—is that a hospital gown? Herbert. It can't be Halloween already, can it? We have no candies, not since you ate the last of the Snickers, you tub of—"

"Marie, it's *March.*"

She doesn't seem to hear. "Goodness me, is that—"And then she's outside, slapping her husband on the back of the head.

"You are strutting around in your underwear waving a gun about in the presence of a *baby*? Have you completely lost it? Do you want to turn the poor thing into Hannibal Lecter?"

To us, smiling: "Honies, who are you? What in the world are you doing here at this hour?"

Jess and Tommy are at a loss for words, so I say, "My name is, uh, Nigel, and this, err, this is my girlfriend," I say, nodding at Jess.

"Ex-girlfriend," Jess corrects.

"Ex-girlfriend," I say. Marie raises her eyebrows but says nothing. "And this"—I point to Tommy—"is, er, my brother. And that little guy, over there, he's my son. And we're here, because, uh," and I'm about to say because we're running from the cops, as they want to take back our baby who's technically not ours anymore, but who wants to get technical, and anyway my name's not actually Nigel, *long story.*

"She was in the hospital," Tommy picks up, nodding at Jess. "Jjj—*Nigel,* came to pick her up, since everyone else she knew was either drunk, on vacation, or dead, but Nigel forgot to bring clothes from her house, which is why she's still in that gown. Also Nigel printed map directions from Yahoo Maps instead of Google Maps, so we got lost and frustrated. We're very sorry for waking you up."

"Oh, honies," she says, and puts a hand to her heart, the hand that's not holding the second shotgun, that is.

"The effort is what counts. That's the thought that's kept me with Herbert all these years, at any rate. I remember I was in the hospital with a broken toe one time and he—"

"Marie, maybe now's not the best time—"

"Shut up, Herbert. Anyway, Herbert, what does he do to make me feel better? He buys me a pair of new shoes. My toe is swollen up to the size of his fat head, and he buys me new shoes."

"They were supposed to motivate you to get better," Herbert mumbles.

"Men," she says, as if she hasn't heard. "God knows I love them, but sometimes I think I should've been a lesbian."

"Marie—"

"But look at me, yammering on with you lot standing out here in the middle of the night! Will you come in?" Her voice is gentle.

We exchange glances. Jess coughs, except her cough sounds like *ahemNOahem*. Tommy nods his head ever so slightly in the direction of his truck.

"You can even spend the night if you want. We have plenty of room." What little common sense I have is practically screaming at me. I should decline, thanks but no thanks, but I can't get the hope in Marie's voice out of my head. And behind us, there's that forlorn little playground.

"Okay," I say to Marie.

Tommy and Jess look at me like I'm insane. *Again.* I thought we'd already settled that.

Marie ushers us into the house, fluttering around like a three-hundred-pound butterfly. She seats us on a couch in the tiny living room. Herbert stands there, bleary-eyed, like he doesn't know where to put himself. Marie heads out of view, calling, "I'll be right back. I'll make us all a good pot of tea."

Tommy puts an arm around my shoulder and leans in to whisper. "If they turn out to be serial killers, I'm going to kill you, Jack."

"Me, too," Jess mutters under her breath.

"You guys are paranoid." To Socrates, though, I say, "Never ever *ever* come inside a house if a crazy old couple carrying shotguns invites you to."

"And what's up with *Nigel*?" Tommy asks.

"You're just mad because you have a generic name," I whisper back. We needn't really whisper, though. Considering the fuss Socrates is now making, we have a better chance of going deaf than of being overheard.

"I'll be right back," I say. Ignoring Tommy and Jess's WTF expressions, I run out to the truck and grab Socrates's stuff. I've only just returned and watched Jess lay him down in his basket, real gentle, when Marie yells out from somewhere unseen.

"Herbert! Get over here. Help me with this—"

The old man throws us a shrug and heads out of the room, mumbling to himself. Together the couple hauls in a small table and plops it down in front of the couch we're sitting on. They go off once more, Herbert returning with a chair in each hand, chairs that look improbably small for their task, and Marie, with a teakettle. Herbert just barely manages to set the chairs down when Marie turns on him.

"You plan on making our guests drink tea out of their hands or were you just going to get some cups? Maybe put some clothes on, for god's sake!"

"I could use a pill or three," he says, and shuffles off.

"You're on enough of those as it is," Marie calls after him. "Anymore and you'll be a walking pharmacy, put Rite Aid round the corner out of business. Or keep them in business, I guess."

Herbert returns with cups but not the right ones. "No, not *those* blue ones, that's copper lettering—are you going blind or deaf here, I can't tell which, because I sure as heck know I said *gold*."

Eventually, the five of us are sitting around the transplanted kitchen table, sipping tea from blue cups with, indeed, very pretty gold lettering. The tea feels good. Sitting in a house, drinking tea with Jess and Tommy and this crazy old couple feels nice. Most of all, what's nice is Socrates, sleeping in his basket.

*Sweet dreams, buddy.*

"I wonder what newborns dream of," I say.

"Probably he's dreaming about what it'll be like to grow up," Jess says, quiet. "Isn't that what all kids dream about? Growing up?"

"And then you grow up, and all you dream about is how you were once young," Herbert says, downs his tea like a shot, and thumps his cup on the table. "Hit me, Marie."

Marie obliges. "I dream about how *you* were once young," she says to Herbert.

"Shut up, Marie," Herbert says.

I am so very tired and the house feels so very warm and peaceful. Something as simple as turning into a driveway, taking the left fork in the road, walking along the road less traveled by, determines where you sleep that night, and where you sleep that night determines the entire adventure, the entire journey, changes the entire universe! My cynical side is like, *not with that universe-changing shit again.* The rest of me though, the romantic in me, is boggled at how going to sleep is like a grain of sand in the Sahara being swept up by the night wind—come morning, the grain of sand is in a different place, and the three and a half million square miles of the Sahara are different for it.

We sit in quiet until I notice a picture of a plump boy on the wall. "Is that your son?" I ask.

Herbert seems taken aback by the question.

"No, dear," Marie says. "Our nephew. Used to live in this area and visit us a lot, when he was little." She smiles. "He loved our little playground. Herbert spent a whole week setting it up, you should've seen him, turning those assembly instructions every which way! I don't know if there's such a thing as dyslexia for diagrams, but if there is, Herbert's got it."

I expect Herbert to tell Marie to shut up. Instead he says, "Wanted to have a kid, that's why I put the playground up in the first place, but it didn't, Marie couldn't—" He downs his second cup of tea, breathes out with a sigh.

"Anyway, he was like a son to us, Jimmy was. Loved the little playground."

"Does he still live in the area?" I ask.

Herbert shakes his head. "No, he's moved away. To California. Has a job and a girl there. Calls on the holidays."

Marie and Herbert wish us good night, and take Jess upstairs to get her a change of clothes. Tommy says something about moving the truck around back and slips out, so I use the opportunity to wash up a bit in the bathroom, run my hands under warm water for a minute or two. Out of the corner of my eye, I catch Jess standing in the doorway in sweatpants and this absurdly big T-shirt. For a while I pretend not to notice. She watches me, head tilted to the side against the doorframe, mouth open a bit like she's about to yawn.

"So you really signed him away? Back there in the hospital? Like, he's really not ours anymore? At all?"

"Was he ever *ours* to begin with, Jack?"

I turn off the faucet, grab a hand towel, and dry my hands, my dripping face.

"You didn't have me sign anything," I say. "Shouldn't

I have signed something?" She looks down, away from my gaze.

"Maybe now's not the best time to have this conversation, Jack. I'm tired."

"Jess."

She shakes her head. "You know I still can't fucking believe you told them you were the biological father." She doesn't sound angry. She sounds tired.

"I can't fucking believe you said you didn't know who the father was!"

"What did you expect, Jack?" Her voice is soft. "He's been *in me* for nine months. You weren't even there. Of fucking course I told everyone that I didn't know who the father was—like some slut. So thanks for that, too, Jack."

"I tried, Jess," I say. "I tried to see you but you wouldn't—"

"That doesn't even matter anymore, Jack," she says. "You can't keep him, you know that, right?"

"I know," I say. I know Socrates will be better off with a normal family, growing up with some boring-ass normal name like John and not being bounced between two barely-out-of-high-school parents whose Facebook relationship status reads, "It's complicated." I'm eighteen fricking years old. What do I know about being a father? What do either of us know about being parents? Yet I ask anyway: "There's no way to make it work, you think? You and me and him?"

"Jack. Don't you think he deserves a normal life? With parents who are committed to each other? Who know where they're going in life? Who have *jobs*, for Christ's sake? You're still in *high school*."

"His new parents might be normal, whatever that means. But they won't be his *real* parents, Jess."

"Real parents have kids when they're ready for them, Jack. His parents will give him things we can't. He'll grow up having a backyard to play in, with friends in the neighborhood whose houses he can walk to. Maybe he'll have a dog. He'll have toys and games and nice clothes, go to a nice school. He'll have after-school activities, play sports; he'll get tutoring if he needs it. Can you give him *any* of that? Can you give him any of that from some freshie dorm next year?"

There's this burning feeling in my heart and I want to say, I want to say so badly, *I can give him Troy!* I can give him stories! I can guide him into his dreams. That's something, isn't it? "I think you're scared," I say.

She smiles. "I'm terrified. I'm afraid to look at him. But then, you're just as scared. You just show it by being outrageously idiotic."

"I can ask my parents, you know. I can ask my parents to take him."

"You don't really mean that, Jack."

She's right. Socrates doesn't deserve to grow up in a house with parents who only agreed to raise him as a favor to their screw-up of a son. But the more I look at her staring back at me with that goddamn patronizing smile, in that stupid oversized T-shirt, the more I want to kiss her. Maybe more than just kiss her. Only Jess can patronize and out-argue you while half-conscious.

"*No*, Jack," she says. "Sometimes I wonder if that's all you boys ever think about."

"I wasn't—" I don't bother continuing. I totally *was*. "What are they like, anyway? His parents. "

"They seemed nice," she says. "The dad's an accountant. The mom's an engineer. They met at their college's math club."

I feel suddenly sick. Good thing the toilet is only a couple feet away.

My expression must've given me away. She says, "I'm

just kidding. It was actually chess club, I think."

I take a step toward her, and her smile fades.

"*Jack*," she says. "I told you, I can barely stand."

"You followed me *all the way* to the bathroom just to *talk?*"

"If by *all the way* you mean I took three steps down the hall, then yeah, I did. To talk . . . alone. Without your boyfriend participating. You two really are cute together, by the way."

"Thanks, Jess," I say. "We think so, too."

"If it doesn't work out for you two, you'll have to hook me up with him."

"Well, there was certainly some chemistry between you two back in the truck. Of a nuclear order. I could feel the atoms splitting."

"Oh, what's a split atom or two?" Jess says. "There are so many."

I give her a meaningful look, to show her I'm having none of this new direction in our conversation. "He joined the army," I say. "Deploying in a couple months for training. To Wyoming."

"Wyoming," she repeats.

"Wyoming."

"Well, that's the price you pay for a man in uniform."

It's strange to hear Jess call Tommy a man. I mean, we call each other "man" all the time. Coming from her though, it feels different. Of all the times I've called Tommy "man," I've never really meant it, never really thought of him as one. We've always been boys. Boys will be boys will be boys. Even though he's taller now, his voice deeper, to me he's still that kid who befriended me my first day at a new school. When do you stop thinking of your best friend as a boy? Of yourself as a boy? I want to go and ask Tommy this—it seems to me, at this moment, very important. I won't, though. You can't just go and ask people the questions that matter most—that would be too easy.

"Thinking deep thoughts, Jack?" Jess knows how to read me too well. Then she adds, "About men in uniforms?"

"Something like that," I say.

We head back to the living room together. Tommy's sprawled out on the couch, near Socrates's basket. He raises an eyebrow at me and I raise an eyebrow at him, and he says, "I couldn't help overhearing. Something about accountants in Wyoming undergoing nuclear reactions."

"Man," I say, with a hand on the couch. "Have I ever

told you your hearing is, like, catlike?"

"Not that I can recall, no."

"Well, get ready."

"Okay," he nods. "Should I sit down for this?"

"A sitting position would be preferable."

"Right," he says, and gets into a sitting position. "I'm—give me a second—just one second. Okay. Ready. Give it to me Jack."

"Tommy—"

"*Give it to me Jack!*"

"Your hearing. It's, like, cat-like and all."

"Yeah, I know dude, you tell me all the time. Make such a big deal of it, too."

Jess rolls her eyes at us. "You two really should get a room."

"Not a bad idea, college girl," Tommy says, and winks at me.

I wink back.

"Speaking of bad ideas," Jess says. "Do you really think we should sleep here?"

"Well, we could probably make good time at night . . ." Tommy says.

"We can't just leave," I say. *Not without saying good-bye.*

"Sure we can. Easy as leaving a hospital with a baby," Jess says.

"We *can't*. I'm exhausted. So is Tommy. So are you— you just told me you can hardly stand."

"I won't have to stand if we drive."

"And for the record, Tommy is not exhausted. Tommy is in prime physical condition for clandestine operations involving kidnapped babies. He's just a little winded, that's all," says Tommy.

"Let's just sleep," I say.

We fall asleep on the couch, on each other, me leaning against Tommy's shoulder, Jess curled into a fetal position with her head against my stomach. Feels good. Until we wake up to Socrates crying his head off. "I got him," I mumble, and shuffle my way over to Socrates in the dark. "I got him."

My dream was something between a nightmare and memory.

Pills.

The feel of them in my mouth.

*But I didn't actually do it.*

Smooth against my tongue, against the roof of my mouth.

Tilting my head back.

*I didn't, I didn't—*

Eyes closed.

Swallow.

Repeat until the eyes stay closed.

Until there is no more meeting a kid named Tommy on my first day at John Bapst—he came over to me and started talking and never quite stopped. No more of him dropping out of our "pretentious private bullshit academy" to go to an "underfunded public moron factory" in a bid to support the "collectivization of educational resources for the general consumption of the proletariat." And no Jess, either—no clinking disposable plastic cups filled with beer or text arguments or unanswered messages or useless apologies or doors shut in my face.

Smooth against my tongue, against the roof of my mouth.

The water cold as it went down.

The boy in the shower, singing a ridiculous song.

*The boy was there, but I didn't.*

I didn't, but I would have, if Jess hadn't called. I hold Socrates in the dark, and shudder.

A long time ago—must've been around third grade—I asked my Dad why he didn't have many friends. *Any,* really, aside from Mom. He told me very few people find a friend they keep through life. That true friendship, the kind the whims of life cannot break, cannot stop or limit, true friendship of this sort, you will probably find only once, and then only if you're lucky.

"That's why people get married," he said. "Because when they think they've found that person they never want to lose him or her."

I wish I could marry Tommy and Jess. Because what we're doing now, what we've done, it all seems so important. But how important can it be if it doesn't keep us together?

I want to explain some of this to Socrates, about friendship and loss, to prepare him for it somehow, like my father tried to do with me. I can't, though, I'm failing him again, I've too much fog in my mind, am too tired, my eyes are heavy and I don't even know if language has the tools for the task.

*"Have you ever considered—have you ever thought of the pain of loss as an affirmation of being* alive *and of having something to* lose?*"* he asks.

"That reminds me," I tell him. "Of this philosopher Mr. Fox quoted once, who says love is a state of willed vulnerability. By loving, you open yourself up to getting hurt, to the pain of loss. Maybe the very act of living—every step we take that carries us farther from some and closer to others—is an act of love?

*"My God. Do you hear yourself? You're more of a romantic than the guy who wrote* 27 Dresses.*"*

I sigh, but don't protest. Won't be long now till I add *27 Dresses* to my DVD collection, right beside *The Notebook* and *Pokémon: The First Movie—Mewtwo vs. Mew.*

I repeat the process of feeding and changing Socrates a few more times during the night. But which of these is dream and which is real? Once I think Jess tells me she'll get Socrates, that I should go back to sleep. Another time I tell her I'll get him, tell her to go back to her dreams. She says okay, and brings her lips to my cheek.

I wake on the floor, curled around Socrates's basket. On the couch, Jess has somehow managed to get her feet up to within inches of Tommy's—at that moment, quivering—nose, which finally gives way to a tremendous sneeze. The spray of snot hits the back of Jess's foot. Jess jolts as if pricked and reflexively pulls a Chuck Norris on Tommy, roundhouse kicking him in the face and off the couch. Tommy's eyes flutter open, and he looks at me in a daze, his hand absently rubbing his bleeding nose.

Jess, comfortable as can be, rolls over onto her stomach and stretches her feet out all the way.

Perhaps Tommy's brain is still in boot-up, still in the first stages of processing the actuality of his existence, in a strange home, on a strange floor, with a bleeding nose brought on by crouching-tiger-sleeping-dragon over there, because he manages only a half-hearted "Bitch."

Marie and Herbert serve us breakfast. Marie forgets the juice and runs off to fetch it faster than I imagined possible. "Always forgetting something," she says as she approaches light speed (but, it is important to note, she does not actually reach light speed, because, as Einstein observed, an object with mass cannot match/surpass the speed of an object without mass, namely, a particle of light).

"Never cooks like this for me," Herbert confides with a grunt.

"Cooking is an art, and art takes inspiration," Marie yells from the kitchen.

"Don't even remember the last time I ate something non-microwavable," Herbert says, and bites into a piece of French toast. "Toast even has *strawberries* on it.

"*Strawberries,*" he repeats, and shakes his head. "Like a real restaurant. Like an—like an IHOP. A real breakfast. *Strawberries.*"

Jess picks at her plate, half asleep, while Tommy wolfs down scrambled eggs, bacon, French toast, and waffles before turning to a grilled-cheese sandwich. My eyes stray to the photo of their nephew again.

"Do you—uh, do you have guests often?" I ask.

Herbert chews on the inside of his cheek and says, "New neighbors stopped by 'bout a month and a half ago because I mowed part of their lawn and they told me they like it natural. Been mowing that part for thirty years. Old neighbors always said thank you."

"What happened to the old neighbors, if you don't mind me asking?" I say.

Herbert hesitates, but only barely. "Old man Baker hit his head while taking a shower and drowned. Wife sold the house, used the money she got from that and his life insurance to buy a place in Florida. She sent us a postcard. A nice postcard. Had a palm tree on it. Always wanted to see a palm tree. She has a new boyfriend now. Young one, sixty-nine, she wrote."

Marie returns with pretty much every juice known to

man, from grapefruit to pineapple to mango. There's not enough room on the table for everything, so she makes a line of the bottles on the floor next to us. I pour myself some mango juice and sip. And sip. And sip.

Maybe they let us in here, three strangers and a baby, into their house, so we could be their kids for a little while.

# 7

## Revelations in a Church Bathroom

The playground grows smaller and smaller through the back window. Herbert and Marie wave, we wave back.

God, I don't know if you exist or not, you probably don't, but in the unlikely event that you do, and in the unlikely event that you care, please send Herbert and Marie more guests. If for no other reason than no human being should have to subsist solely on microwavable food. *Amen.*

We pause at the end of their driveway while Tommy programs 7 Birch Street, Clifford, New York, into the GPS. Then he turns onto the road, accelerating, and we leave Marie and Herbert behind.

"How long?" Jess asks.

"Well. The straightest route would take us five and a half hours to get to Lake Champlain. And Clifford's way on the other side of the lake." Tommy pauses. "But, I think we should keep to the back roads. Less of a chance to bump into the cops that way."

"So?" Jess says.

"Well. I mean—the estimate assumes we'll be going the speed limit. We're not going to be going the speed limit."

"How long, Tommy?" Jess says.

"About eight hours just to get to Lake Champlain. Add a few hours more on to that to get to Clifford."

"That's assuming we don't get lost," Jess says.

"We have a GPS," Tommy says. "What could go wrong?"

"Your GPS doesn't even speak *English*."

"Oh, relax, Jess," I say. "We're still alive. We'll be fine."

"Oh, well, thank you, Jack," she says, turning to face me. "Now that I know we'll be fine, that just, well, by golly that puts my twittering heart right at ease."

We're in the back together with Socrates. I have some doubts as to her devotion to The Cause. Also I want to kiss her so much it hurts. But does she want to kiss me back? Or will she just try to run off first chance she gets? It's like she knows what I'm thinking, though. She meets my eye and says, "Look, as long as Jason Statham behind the wheel over there remembers this isn't the next *Transporter*, I promise not to do anything too crazy. Even though this *is* crazy." Under her breath, she mutters something about a German-speaking GPS.

"Hey, Jason Statham's got nothing on me," Tommy says. "I learned to drive by playing *Grand Theft Auto* and watching *The Fast and the Furious*, not by being a glorified package-delivery man and bona fide bitch. *Transporter,* my ass."

"And a fine one it is," I say, eager to change the subject and stop their arguing, even if the subject we're changing to is Tommy's ass. Still, Jason Statham probably didn't fail the practical portion of his driving test three times. I can almost hear Tommy's response—*Parallel frickin' parking, man!*

"You guys are so. Weird," Jess says. "And the only thing *Grand Theft Auto* ever taught anyone was to shoot hookers to get your money back."

"Oh, chair-throwing college-girl, how you wound me

with your narrow-sightedness. In *Grand Theft Auto* you have a virtual city of virtual people following a set of rules—go this fast, do this, don't do that—with consequences if they deviate from the specified norms of appropriate behavior. And the beautiful thing is, you get to blow those rules to high hell. You get to rocket-launcher them to pieces. What you have—"

I've already heard Tommy's lecture on how *Grand Theft Auto* actualizes on the human need to create chaos to usurp the dystopic totalitarianism of all ordered systems, so I divert my attention from his lovely voice to getting my cell phone out of my pocket. By now my parents probably know what's going on, so I should at least make an effort to prevent them from having brain hemorrhages. Actually getting the phone out, though, proves a more difficult undertaking than it should, what with us sitting down and the phone sandwiched between my wallet and my leg. Finally, I get a grip on it, but that's only half the battle. Now I need to work both my hand and my phone out. Jess catches my struggle, and her eyes narrow.

"Are you—are you *pulling* yourself right next to the *baby?*" she says, and covers Socrates's eyes with one hand.

"What—no—I'm trying to—"

"You guys suck," Tommy says. "I'm talking to you about what's at the very core of human nature, case in point, *Grand Theft Auto*, and Jack's too busy jacking off—wait a minute, that's hilarious. Jack jacking off. Ha. Wait, what's that noise?"

Ringing. My pants are ringing. I try to stop it, but a second later my mom's frantic voice is coming out of my pants. "HELLO? HELLO? Honey, is that you? HELLO?"

"Mom?" I say, as I lean in toward my crotch.

"Oh my God, honey, we've called so many times and the police have been here, and what's going on? What's going on? They said something about a baby. Honey? Honey, whatever is going on, you can tell me—I can't hear you very well—where are you? What are you doing?"

"We're fine, Mom. We're all right."

I've given up trying to get my cell out, but it must be on speakerphone—I hear my mom well enough to know she's hyperventilating.

"We? Honey? Who's we? Honey?"

Oops. "Er, the baby and I."

"Honey, what are you doing with a baby? You have to give him back. Are you listening to me? Why did you even—what possessed you to—you have to give him back now, Jack, before you ruin your whole life—" The longer she talks, the higher in pitch her voice gets. Soon only dogs will be able to hear her.

"HONEY?" she says before I have a chance to respond. "Honey? Honey, are you there? Are you listening to me? You have to—" I don't want to hear what I "have to." I jam on my phone, pressing as many buttons as I can through the fabric of my jeans.

Hit the END key. Let me hit the goddamn END key.

Finally, I do. We drive in quiet. I want to laugh. That or bang my head against the window.

"Jack, buddy?" says Tommy.

"Yeah."

"Next time you want to pull voices out of your pants, could you maybe give me some advance notice? Scared the crap out of me."

"Sorry," I say, and smile.

"And Jack, darling?" Jess says.

"Yeah?"

"While we're on the subject of what goes on in your pants—"

"I wasn't—"

"I know you weren't, darling, and next time you're not

jacking off, don't not do it in front of my baby, okay?"

Her baby. *Her* baby. I feel indignant at how indignant she sounds.


We pull into the small town of Harmony to fill up on gas. Tommy stops at the one and only gas station. While he takes care of the gas and stocks up on snacks, I grab Socrates out of his car seat and walk along the lonely, winding road with the little guy pressed against my shoulder. There are these great northern pines, casting everything, from the grass to the pavement to the gas station to the run-down, one-story homes, into shadow. Off in the distance, mountains rise to meet a dark gray horizon. A cool breeze blows as the occasional car travels in and out of our lives at ten miles over the speed limit.

"The right road can lead you anywhere," I say. "All you need is a driver's license. And a car. And gas, as you can see." I nod at Tommy, filling up. "But in theory. Anywhere, Socrates. Anywhere at all. Just imagine it. And of course, road and car and gas and a driver's license aren't literal. A road doesn't have to be a road, and a car doesn't have to be a car, you know? Just like a ceiling doesn't have to be a ceiling and Troy doesn't have to be Troy. It can be anything. Like, for Jason and the Argonauts on their quest for the Golden Fleece, the *Argo* was their car and the seas their road." So he doesn't take my comparison to Jason and the Argonauts too literally, I clarify. "Which is not to say you should expect to face sirens and fire-breathing oxen. I mean, you will, but they won't really be sirens and fire-breathing oxen. We all have our own fire-breathing oxen, just like we all have our own Golden Fleeces, which don't have to be gold or fleeces at all!"

I'm not making any sense again. I just—

"*What's your Golden Fleece, then?*" Socrates asks.

"Well," I say, and hesitate. What *is* my golden fleece? What is it I'm after? To say good-bye? Or maybe Jess is right. Maybe I'm hoping something magical will happen, and I won't have to say good-bye. Maybe that's my golden fleece. But if that's what it is, then the fleece is little more than a dream. And dreams always fade as soon as you open your eyes.

Footsteps from behind. Jess falls in next to me and saves me from having to give Socrates an answer. We walk a bit together, and before I can stop myself, I ask, "What do you think he'll be like? When he grows up, I mean."

"I don't know." She throws Socrates a brief glance.

"He has your eyes," I say, even though looks aren't what I really meant.

"Jack, they all have blue eyes at this age."

"Not the color. He has this—like a twinkle sort of thing." We stop and I hold him up to her face. "See?" Then, "You have it, too, sometimes."

Jess looks away.

"Everyone's eyes twinkle, Jack," she says, as we start walking again.

"But not in the same *way*."

She doesn't reply, just gives me this wistful smile. So I say, "He's going to be a philosopher you know."

Jess rolls her eyes, laughs. "With a name like that, what choice have you given him?"

She's got me there. But I'm serious. I want to tell her he's going to change the universe and ponder the universe as he changes it, that his pondering the universe *will* change the universe, has changed it already. I don't though. She'll tell me I'm crazy. *Again.*

"It's hard, you know," I say, and mean it. "Thinking about things you'll probably never get answers to. Like when my parents called to tell me my dog got hit by a car—I was really sad for a day or two. But little by little

I stopped thinking about her and that's how I got over it. But if he's a philosopher, he'll never really get over things. Never really stop thinking."

"I don't think that's a philosopher thing, Jack. I think that's a human thing. Not everyone who thinks about—I'm quoting to the best of my ability here, as you were slurring your words a bit—'the chafing chains of determinism and the folly of free will' does so aloud, to a room full of stoned college kids. In fact, I'm not even sure that's a philosopher thing so much as a Jack thing."

"I did not call the chains *chafing.*"

"That's what it sounded like, but like I said—"

"Yeah, yeah, I got it," I say, annoyed at Jess for being right. But Socrates, he whispers, *"You're* both *right. It's human to wonder, because all humans are philosophers!"*

"If we are human, then we wonder. Philosophers wonder. Therefore all humans are philosophers. That's a logical fallacy. You're affirming the consequent."

"Jack. You're starting to worry me." Jess says.

"Oh—sorry," I say. To Socrates, *"Thanks for that."*

*"No problem—what are voices-in-your-head for? Also, try a different formulation. Philosophy is the act of wondering at the world. If we wonder at the world, then we engage in philosophy."*

Up a ways we see what looks like a house with—I squint—yes, a cross on top. From the gas station Tommy yells, "Hey! Calling America's Newest Hyper-dysfunctional family. The truck's ready! And MTV called. They want to do a show. They want to put you on after *Engaged & Underage*."

"Oh my God. I *love Engaged & Underage*," I yell back.

"I can see it now," Jess says. "They'll call it *Stealing Socrates*. If it does well they might do a spinoff series—*Raising Socrates*."

"You coming or not?" Tommy's yelling. "Also you should make me your agent! There's nothing I want more than to exploi—I mean support you in this endeavor."

"Done. But we're not going yet. Come here. I want to—I think I want to go to church."

Yes. Multimillion-dollar deals with MTV aside, it feels right—talking about what it means to be human one minute and stumbling on a church the next. What's more human than believing in something, having a church of your own, whether it be the house of Jesus with a capital J or that of the Flying Spaghetti Monster? (Praised be His sumptuous noodles, from whence all creation came.)

"Are you sure you're okay?" Jess says.

She is right to be concerned. My wanting to go to church is strange for a number of reasons, up to and including the fact that I'm Jewish. I quicken my pace and don't try to explain.

"Dude," Tommy says, running up from behind us. "I don't think I heard you right. I was all like 'MTV called' and then I heard you say something crazy about going to church."

"I was standing right next to him, and I can't believe it either," Jess says.

"Come on, guys," I say. And I'm walking up a small hill, toward the little building, Socrates against my shoulder.

"Dude. I can't go in there, man. Do you know what they do to people like me? Do you want me to end up like Joan of Arc?"

"Joan of Arc," I say, "was burned for being a witch. You're an atheist. I believe they'll give you a chance to change your mind before resorting to that. Now come on."

"You're Jewish, man," he says as we draw nearer. "*Jewish*. Are you really going to betray your people like that?"

"I just want Socrates to see . . ."

"See what?" he says.

What, indeed?

At the top of the hill I push through the front door of the church and into a tiny room crammed with wooden benches. There's nobody around. Tommy and Jess look at me like I'm the wicked witch of the west and Alice—no, sorry, *Dorothy* just broke a jug of water over my head.

"Just give me a second," I say. I bring Socrates up to the front bench, sit down, and take a deep breath. Press him close, so I have his head resting against my lips.

I whisper, "Remember that conversation we had about ceilings? Before Tommy interrupted us? And you said we had to believe in a ceiling to end all ceilings? Well, some people think God created the first ceiling, which was the universe. And next he created another ceiling—our world."

I pause. Then tell him, "I used to believe that god was the creator of ceilings. Bob taught me that, and when I asked her why she believed in him, she said, 'There's so much beauty in the world.'" I tell my son what I could never tell Bob. "I think the problem of the ceilings and beginnings can't be solved that easily. If you want someone to create the first ceiling, make someone responsible for the beginning of everything, fine, but you run into the problem of, well, who created the guy who created that first thing—the universe? And if you say *nobody* created God, well, that's basically the same problem we had before . . . And if you say the guy created himself, that he's self-creating, then that's kind of cheating, you know? Why can't the universe be self-creating, then?

"So," I say. "So you don't have to believe in God if you don't want to. He doesn't have to be *your* ceiling to end all ceilings. But I think maybe you were right, before. I think you need to believe in *something* above and beyond everything else. Could be Jesus or Zeus or Odin, or maybe it's not God at all, but love or humanity or whatever, but you have to find something; otherwise, what's the point?" I touch the soft hair on his head. "You have to find your own golden fleece, Socrates. It's not important whether the fleece turns out to be real or whether you ever get your hands on it. What's important is to have something to quest for. Otherwise you're just moving from point A to point B. Otherwise Harmony's a little out-of-the-way town nobody cares about. But we know it's not, we know it's more than that, because out of all the places in the world, the universe, we're *here*, *now*, on the way to see Bob, and that makes all the difference."

*"What about nihilists?"* Socrates asks. *"Don't they believe in nothing? They don't have a Golden Fleece . . ."*

"Nihilists don't really believe in nothing. They believe in believing in nothing. Their Golden Fleece is that there is no Golden Fleece. The only *true* nihilists are the dead. The living ones are posers."

The bottle of pills. Water steaming from the faucet. Swallow. And swallow. And swallow.

*I didn't do it I didn't.*

I shiver. Who am I trying to convince?

Stop. Stop thinking about it.

But I can't.

Because it happened little more than twenty-four hours ago. Thinking about popping pills and jumping out of windows. Facebook-fueled depression. I don't want to die. Don't even know what death *is*. It's another big question mark, another answer I'll never get. I close my eyes, wait for the world to make sense. For me to make sense. An epiphany or revelation or something would be nice. I'd even settle for a talking fire at this point. I can see it now; descending through the roof and saying, "'Sup? Heard you were talking about me. And ceilings. Thought I'd do a little dropping in. Through a ceiling. Say hello, maybe sign an autograph."

Instead of a talking fire, I get my boy Tommy saying, "I gotta piss. There must be a bathroom here somewhere."

He moves cautiously away from the entrance, looking around.

"Come to think of it, I could go, too." I get up and walk over to Jess, offer up Socrates. "Will you hold him for me while I go?"

"Sure," she says, taking him. She presses him to her breast, brushes a finger through his wisps of hair. "You two have fun now."

The church bathroom resembles a wallpapered closet. It contains a single stall, a yellowed sink, and an old relic of a hand dryer.

Tommy nods at the stall. "Ladies first. And hurry it up. I need to take a tremendous shit."

"Such a gentleman."

Inside the stall I lift up the toilet lid, unzip my pants, and try to make myself take a leak. Nothing comes, and finally I say, "Tommy, I didn't actually come here because I have to piss."

"No?"

"No."

"Well then why the hell am I out here and you in there?"

"Tommy. I think I—I think I might have almost tried to kill myself before. Yesterday, I mean. Or almost tried to almost kill myself. It gets confusing."

"Jack. What are you talking about?"

"Yesterday, Tommy. I may have almost tried to almost kill myself . . ."

"Jack," he finally says. "What do you mean you think you may have almost tried to almost kill yourself? The hell does that even mean? I was *with* you yesterday. We watched fucking Pokémon and you kidnapped a baby. We met Herbie and Marie. We—"

"In the morning. Before Jess called. I was about to pop some pills. A bottle full. Then my cell rang. I think I would've done it, Tommy. If the phone hadn't rang. I think I wanted to almost kill myself."

"Jack. Jack, you've got to be joking. This is a joke. Right?" He laughs nervously.

"No," and that's when the piss comes. Something about my voice must've convinced Tommy of my seriousness—he's gone quiet. There's only the sound of my urine hitting the toilet bowl. I run dry. Flush. Wait. "I got up and saw all these Facebook Happy Birthday messages and I got kind of depressed and thought maybe I could try to almost kill myself. You know? I thought about jumping out a window, but I figured that could end badly because I might cripple or even *actually* kill myself. So I decided on pills."

"Shit, Jack." It scares me how scared he sounds. "Shit, Jack. Why?"

The "why" throws me off guard.

"And how the hell"—his voice is higher than I've ever heard it before—"do you try to *almost* kill yourself, huh, man? How do you almost—almost—"

I hear a soft thump. I open the stall door to see Tommy slumped down on the dirty hardwood floor, looking up at me. I sit down next to him.

"Don't you ever get really depressed about stuff?" For me, "stuff" roughly translates to: life and death, how everyone seems to be going in different directions and the fear that you will end up alone and nobody will notice you're alive when you're alive and gone when you're gone.

"Yeah, man. Yeah. But I don't. I don't try and kill myself."

"And then there's the ceilings and infinity and God and not having free will."

"Jack. What *are* you talking about?"

"I don't know," I say, but I do. I do know. It gets so lonely in a world that might not have meaning or purpose or God, a world that might not make any sense at all. I settle for, "You know how the universe is infinite, right?"

Tommy just nods, and I think I love him for it.

"So we can think of the earth as a soccer ball, and the galaxy as a gigantic soccer field, and we know that outside our soccer field are billions and billions of other soccer fields, all traveling in different directions from the center of the universe and making the universe expand with them, or maybe they're entering a new universe, who really knows." I pause. "Right?"

"Right."

"Now let's stop thinking about the infinite universe or infinite universes—which would really make it one big infinite multiverse, and go back to the soccer ball. Our soccer ball. So each black hexagon—"

"Pentagon."

"Right. Each black hexagon or pentagon or whatever is like a place on earth, and we're little ants crawling around the surface of the soccer ball, and we've been kicked, and we're just sort of crawling around on the surface and we're so small, we're like bits of glass caught in hurricane winds—"

"Christ, Jack, settle on a metaphor already—"

"We're like bits of glass caught in hurricane winds," I say louder, "and we're always flying away from each other, we're always crawling away from each other on our soccer ball, and why do we do that? Why do we do that when we're all flying through space going sixty-seven thousand miles per hour round and round the sun, six hundred thousand miles per hour through the galaxy, one point three million miles per hour through the infinite universe, and who knows how fast through whatever's beyond that?"

"I—I don't know, Jack. But how is killing yourself going to solve anything?"

"But that's just it. I didn't really want to kill myself. I—I don't know. It sounds stupid, but I only wanted people to come visit me. You know? When I got my appendix out and all my family came to visit and kids from my school wrote me Get Well notes and you came and stayed the whole day and we played Golden-eye. I don't know, I felt like people actually cared, like for a little while the ants all visited my hexagon."

"Pentagon."

"Right, and then I got out and everything was back to normal. The kids who wrote me the cards didn't speak to me since we weren't actually ever friends. You were still at your stupid new school. I went back to seeing relatives once every six months. I don't know. I thought—I know it's selfish, but I just wanted people to remember me for a while again. I felt like, after I broke up with Jess, I didn't have—" I can't bring myself to finish, to say *have anyone.*

"Was it my fault?" he asks.

"No, man," I say. "I was—depressed. Dude, how could it have been your fault? You're my best friend. If not for you, I'd probably have really been trying to kill myself, instead of trying to almost kill myself."

"Don't joke, Jack."

But that's the thing—I'm not at all sure I'm joking.

"And if you say *almost* one more time—" he continues.

A knock on the door makes us both jump. "I didn't think you two would take my encouragement so seriously," Jess says. "You going to be out anytime soon, or should I get comfortable?"

"We're coming," I say.

"You sure you're okay in there?"

"Yeah," Tommy says.

"Yeah," I say. "We'll be out in a minute, Jess. Just— just give us a minute."

"Okay, Jack," she says, real gentle.

"Does she know? About you—" Tommy whispers.

"No. She'd freak."

He snorts. "I'm freaked, Jack. You need to, like, I dunno, talk to someone or something. *Fuck*, man. *I* need to talk to someone about you needing to talk to someone."

"I'm sorry."

"Who the fuck tries to almost kill himself, anyway? You start explaining it, talking about soccer balls and hurricanes, and for a few seconds it almost kind of makes a weird sort of sense, but the second you stop talking I realize how fucking crazy it is. Like, here, get me a gun, I'm going to try and almost shoot my brains out and onto a nearby wall. What the *fuck*, man?" He coughs, gives the trash can a half-hearted kick.

"I don't want to die, Tommy." I start to pick at the peeling wallpaper.

"Promise me. Promise me you mean it. Promise me you won't try to kill, or almost kill, or do whatever you were trying to almost do to yourself ever again."

I meet his gaze and quickly look away. His eyes are wet and I don't want to embarrass him.

"Look at me, man. And promise."

I look at him and say, "I promise," and I mean it.

He clears his throat. "Okay. Okay then." He pushes himself up, offers me a hand. I take it, turn the faucet on, rinse my hands, reach for the hand dryer.

"Broken," he says.

"Should've figured." I turn toward him, the tiniest semblance of a grin creeping onto my face. "Don't," he says, but I've already flicked my hands, the little drops of water already raining on his face.

"Son-of-a—" He's grinning now, too, and reaches for the faucet. I intercept him and we struggle against each other. He's bigger, though, and pushes me into the wall, turns the water back on, and splashes me. I duck and tackle him into the door. We're locked in mortal combat until he says, "Dude, I've really got to take that tremendous shit now." Almost simultaneously, we stop, disentangle ourselves. He shoulders past me on his way to the stall, intentionally bumping me, and shuts the door before I can retaliate.

"I win," he calls from what he thinks is safety.

I turn on the faucet, and fill my hands with water.

He knows what's coming. "If you do, I swear, Jack, I will—"

I send the handful up and over the side of the stall.

The last thing I hear before I run out of the bathroom is "Bastard!"

# 8

## Pancakes with Homer

We eat lunch at the local Pancake Palace, where they promise to have "the best pancakes around." Far as I can see, they have the only pancakes around. But I admire them for using a word like "around." Lots of places boast of having the best this or that in the county or the state or the world, and you eat there and it's like no, no, you don't. "Around," though, "around" is the kind of word that you can make as big or small as you see fit.

The server looks us over, adjusts her glasses, sees we're still there, grunts, seats us, hands out menus that could pass for books. The smell of sugar and butter and syrup makes me think of breakfast at Bob's, when she'd get up early to make pancakes for me. Eventually I grew tired of them. Maybe it was my taste buds changing. She kept making them for me until one day I told her, "Bob, I don't really like pancakes much anymore." I regretted it the moment I said it, but too late, couldn't take it back. I meet Socrates's eye, then—Jess is feeding him from the bottle—*he understands*. Even though he's only a day old and hasn't hurt anyone yet. The world's so fragile, and we're all so clumsy. But maybe Socrates will be more sure-footed than me.

We leaf through the menu books. There are so many options it's impossible to make a decision. When the time comes to order, I pick something at random and forget what I chose as soon as our server walks away.

Tommy waits till she's gone. "Look, Jack," he says, "there's something I've been thinking about . . . Herbie and Marie were nice and all, but I'm willing to bet they also got kind of curious as to why three kids and a baby showed up at their doorstep. All they'd have to do is make a call or two—probably, out of concern, wanting to look out for us. I don't know if they'd have the storage capacity to remember my license plate number, and even if they do, the data might have gotten corrupted during encryption, but I'm pretty sure they'd remember what my truck looks like. Maybe even the make. And they'd know what direction we headed off in. Plus there's the cop that probably saw my license plate last night."

Jess is staring at Tommy, cheeks bulging. She gulps and says, "So? What do you propose, Mr. *Grand Theft Auto*? And please don't say *Grand Theft Auto*. Accessory to kidnapping is enough for me, thanks."

He gives us a thin smile. "I say we get off the road."

I give him a blank look and he rolls his eyes, says, "Take to the seas. I've checked it all out on the GPS. Clifford is a port town, right on the southwestern bank of Lake Champlain. It's perfect."

"You're not thinking what I think you're thinking."

"That depends. What are you thinking with the hope that I'm not thinking it?"

"Not your dad's—"

"Yes!" He beams at me. For Jess's benefit, he says, "My dad has a yacht moored in St. Albans. On *our* side of Lake Champlain. We're going to borrow it." He sticks his hand in his pocket, produces a pair of keys, and gives them a jingle.

"Do you even know how to—" I start.

"'Course. I haven't sailed in a while, but it'll all come back to me. Like riding a bike. Besides, we've got a manual stowed somewhere on board. Dad never let us sail without it."

I turn to Jess for help. She shrugs. "At this point, I wouldn't be surprised if Grandma turned out to be Baba Yaga and you two lovebirds decided we were going to fly to Siberia. Though I'm curious to know how your parents will react to you stealing their yacht."

"Disown me, I suppose," Tommy says, rather cheerily.

"You know, maybe you and your parents would benefit from one of those family therapy sessions," Jess says.

"Oh, we benefited all right," Tommy says. "Dad ended up sleeping with the therapist, Mom ended up sleeping with the secretary, who was a girl, by the way, and I got lollipops every week for a few months while everyone was getting their therapy on."

"Wow," Jess says.

"Now's your turn," Tommy says, "to tell me how messed up your life is."

"Well, where do I start?" Jess says. "Maybe—oh, I know, yesterday, when my ex-boyfriend—"

"Yeah, okay, Jess," I say. "We get it. Big bad boy-friend—"

"Ex-boyfriend," Jess says. "And you weigh less than me, darling."

"I've put on two and a half pounds of muscle since then."

"No way."

"Yeah, I know. I was impressed, too. Point is—*Tommy and I were there.* We know."

"Anyway what about your family, college girl?" Tommy says. "I mean, don't get me wrong, I'm sure your life is fascinatingly tragic, but what I really want to hear about is your messed-up family. So I can feel better about mine."

"My family is just fine, thanks."

"Jess," I say, "wasn't everyone you knew drunk, on vacation, or dead the day you gave birth?"

Jess snorts. "Drunk, on vacation, dead, or option D, kidnapping my baby—"

"Ouch," Tommy says.

"Ouch," I agree. Leaning in to whisper into Socrates's ear, I say, "Your mother, she just won't let it go. I mean, it's not like I hold the torrent of flying chairs against her."

"Oh, please," Jess says. "Two is hardly a torrent—"

"It's a torrent when it's directed at you," I say.

"—and you make it sound so violent," she continues. "It was more like a toss. A couple gentle tosses."

"Well," Tommy says, "I have to say, my parents and I have our issues. But I can tell you for a fact, a sure fact, that if I were about to give birth, they would totally be there. So whatever their shitty reason was, I'm sorry yours weren't, college girl."

"Yeah, well," Jess says, and doesn't continue.

Tommy finishes his food first, and leans back with his eyes closed. Jess and I take our time. The stacks are huge, and though we pick at them, they don't seem to get much smaller. The server checks in on us begrudgingly, asks "Can I get you anything else?" in a way that makes me think she'll spit in it if I say yes. She brightens considerably when we request the check. "If you have a bit o' spare time you should stop by our local landmark," she tells us. "This town here's proud to be founded right by the world's biggest pebble."

It would be easy to mistake the world's biggest pebble for a boulder. Fortunately, there's a wooden sign next to it, proclaiming it to be, in fact, a pebble. We decide to sit on the world's biggest pebble.

"Well," I say from my perch. "I'm glad we did this."

"Maybe this disproves my theory about how everything we do is causally predetermined," I say to Socrates, whom Jess has been refusing to relinquish. "I mean, kidnapping a baby, or picking my nose in first grade, I can see how those would be predetermined, but a pilgrimage to the world's biggest pebble? That's stretching it. Who even knew there *was* a world's biggest pebble?"

"Jack. Are you *really* talking to the baby about picking your nose in first grade?"

"I—no—I was, you're taking that out of context, Jess."

"Do enlighten me then, darling."

"Well, *dear*, I was telling him about determinism—"

"You know, Jack, on second thought, I think I'll pass." She's smiling though. Reluctantly, but it still counts.

"Now we've done it all," Tommy says. "Eaten the best pancakes, sat on the world's biggest boulder—sorry, pebble. Picked our noses . . ."

"Well, I'm glad you two are enjoying yourselves," Jess says, and rocks Socrates gently.

"I do kinda feel like this whole biggest pebble thing might be a very smart case of false advertising," I say.

"All word of mouth's false, and everything ya see with yer own eyes be true," a cracked voice says as a man walks into view, wearing a brown greatcoat that looks like it functions as a mode of apparel, a form of shelter, and even, from the little bits and pieces missing, perhaps a snack in hungry times.

"I see ya've come to my pebble," he says, and gives us a yellowed grin.

"It-er-is a very nice pebble," I say.

"That she is," the man says.

"I thought it was the town's," Tommy says.

"Pah," the man says, and dismisses that idea with a wave of his hand. "The town. The town. What's a town but a buncha people livin' next t' each other callin' theyselves a town? If tomorra they decided they wasn't a town, that they was just a buncha people livin' next t' each other, then there'd be no more talka town. Just 'cause they's a town today, they think they own m' pebble?" He laughs. We laugh nervously with him.

Tommy leans over and says, "And here he is, ladies and gents, behind invisible door number one, ding-ding-ding-ring-a-ling, crazy number fricking four."

The man gives Tommy a hard look, so to divert crazy

number fricking four's attention, I say, "Do you, uh—live here?"

"I live," the man says, "always here. Never there. Till one day I'll be ever there and never more here, if, that is, there's a there at all." He bursts out laughing again. This time he's alone.

"So why do you call it the world's largest pebble and not just a boulder?" Tommy asks.

"Because then, nobody'd come visit it. How many damn plain old boulders ya think we got in this country o' ours? But we only got one giant pebble." He holds up a single, dirty-nailed finger in emphasis.

His gaze falls on Socrates then, up there with Jess. "Ah," he says, and it's like, with that "ah," he understands everything, knows why we've come to this place, made the pilgrimage to see his pebble. "Ah," he says again. "Been sucha time since I seen one of 'em up close."

The way he says it, it's like he's talking about a rare species of animal, a white-tailed ferret or something. I don't actually know if white-tailed ferrets are rare. Jess tightens her grip on Socrates.

There's an awkward sort of silence, so I ask, "Did you ever have kids of your own?"

"Did I ever have kids of m' own?" he repeats, and looks at the ground.

"Maybe we should go," Jess whispers in my ear. "I think we should go, Jack. *Jack.*"

"No," the man says. "No, I never had a kid of m' own. Fathered some, I think, but never called one of 'em m' own. Never called one of 'em son.

"Do you know why I own this pebble?" he asks. "Do you know why it's mine?"

"Non sequitur," Tommy says under his breath. But the man hears.

"Oh, it follows, boy. Oh, it follows. The pebble is mine because I own the earth. And d'ya know why I own the earth?"

Jess's elbow catches me in the ribs, but I ignore it. I want to know why he owns the earth. Socrates is curious, too, I can tell.

"Why do you own the earth?" I ask for the both of us.

"Why do *you* own the earth?" he says back to me. "You"—he points to Tommy—"and you"—Jess now— "and you"—me now, and—"even you"— he says, and his finger's aimed back at Jess but I know he means Socrates.

"Because yer stardust." He throws up his arms. "Fifteen billion years ago, boom-shaka-bam, the universe and the galaxies and the stars, and from the stars the planets and from the planets the rocks and the pebbles and us. We're all stardust, sparks flying from the fire. We're the same, you, me, and m'pebble, matter assemblin' and reassemblin', and no town, *no town's* a-gonna change that."

We go quiet.

Of course! The ant is not only a part of the soccer ball and the soccer field and the universe, but *has always been* and *will always be* a part of them. And if Nietzsche is right about eternal return then maybe there's an eternal return of matter, an eternal return of all the little individual bits that make up the ant, so that these little bits will come together in precisely the right way to create a new ant, and this will occur an infinite number of times in the future and has occurred an infinite number of times in the past and oh god what is more poetic than that little sideways eight? It's like how Bob told me she wanted to be cremated, have her ashes scattered by a plane, so she could be with me everywhere—in the ground I walk on, the sky I wonder at, the water I drink, and the wind that blows in my face.

I surprise everyone, including myself, by saying, "Do you want to go get something to eat?" We've eaten, but he looks hungry, and experience tells me that crazy takes a lot of calories to sustain. Besides, I want to listen to him talk some more.

The man frowns at me. I'm afraid I've upset him. Slow, cautious, he says, "Pancake Palace?"

"Er—if you want?"

"*Pancake* Palace," he says, and licks his chapped lips. "They say they got the best pancakes around. Never managed to have 'em myself, but they say, they say . . ."

"I don't think this is a good idea," Jess says when the man starts walking to our truck. "Scratch that. I think this is a very bad idea. The worst idea yet, actually, which is saying something."

Tommy, watching the man's back, says, "I think if he were going to try and kill us he'd do it after we fed him. We shouldn't have anything to worry about for the time being."

With that, the matter is settled.

I climb into the back to sit with Jess and Socrates and let stardust man ride shotgun. As he's clambering in I say, "We never caught your name."

"Name's Homer," he says, and pulls the door shut. Tommy guffaws.

"Somethin' funny there, boy?" the man says.

"Oh, don't mind me," Tommy says. "I just never thought I'd have the privilege of being in the company of both Homer and Socrates. At the same time. In my truck. Driving to Pancake Palace."

On the way there, we pass a police car headed in the opposite direction. This sends me into a very mild form of cardiac arrest. I manage to recover by the time we pull into Pancake Palace. Homer enters at least ten strides ahead of us, like he's afraid our offer has an expiration date. He says to the wide-eyed server in a triumphant and booming voice, "Four, please. And a baby." We hear it from outside.

The server appears only marginally relieved once we assemble around Homer. She does seat us, though. I hold Socrates this time.

Tommy, Jess, and I order dessert; milkshakes, to be precise—diners have good milkshakes. Homer says, "Mo' time. I need mo' time." The server purses her lips and goes off to feign business, even though we're the only customers. Homer leafs through the menu's laminated pages in the manner of a priest handling the Holy Writ, mumbling something about pancakes and who knew and Bessie. Bessie sounds like a non sequitur, but I don't say this aloud. Instead, I turn to Socrates, try to share some of my milkshake with him, stick the straw in his mouth, but he doesn't know how to suck it, gives me a WTF expression worthy of an internet meme, and I'm like "Dude, pretend it's a tit and suck." He still doesn't get it. Jess catches us and her eyes go wide. "*Jack*," she says, tone severe. "Don't be an idiot."

Homer ends up going with some towering, blueberry-filled monstrosity complete with whipped cream and a few actual blueberries on top. When he sees the server bringing it, his jaw drops a little, and after she sets it down in front of him, he stares at that leaning tower like he expects it to break out in song. "I'm a Believer," maybe.

Any second now. Any. Second.

When it doesn't, he puts his head in his arms and erupts into tears. The server looks from us to Homer to us to Homer. Homer's shoulders tremble. He inhales sharply, and the server winces. She reaches out a hesitant hand, and pats him on the back a couple times.

"There, there," she says. "It's okay. If you don't finish, you can take it home. In a box."

This only makes him cry harder.

"I think," Tommy says softly, "he's upset at the thought of eating so much stardust. Would be like eating yourself. Or the world's biggest pebble. Or yourself *and* the world's biggest pebble."

I bite back a laugh, but Jess almost chokes on her milkshake and snorts some of it out her nose.

Eventually Homer manages to recover long enough to take a bite. Once he does, he doesn't stop. Forkful follows forkful. He pauses only to come up for air and to sniff occasionally into his lapkin.

"I can't believe you ordered a vanilla milkshake, dude," Tommy says, sipping his own fancy-shmancy chocolate. "How terrifically generic. I expected more from a guy who names his son Socrates."

"Yeah," I say. "Well, sorry to disappoint, mate."

"Dude, Australia is *so* two old farts with shotguns and one giant pebble and Mr. Stardust ago."

"And the sleep-kicking episode," I say.

He gives Jess a hard look. "I don't know how you survived her."

"Oh," Jess says. "It was easy. He never stayed a second too long."

Tommy raises his eyebrows but says nothing. I meet Jess's gaze and immediately want to turn away. There's too much there, and it's all so convoluted.

"I *am* sorry, Jess," I say. "I should've stayed."

"No," she says, resting her head in one hand and looking at me with this sidelong glance. "No," she says. "You shouldn't have. You didn't love me."

Tommy busies himself with admiring his fingernails. They *are* very nice, as fingernails go.

"You didn't love me, so what was there to stay for?" She says it matter-of-factly.

My chest tightens. I want to tell her I do love her. But that would be a lie. I might have then, but now? Or maybe—ah, how should I know? I watch her, and she watches me, and I watch her watching me, and I just don't know.

"How do you know you're in love?" I ask Jess.

She smiles at me—I've missed that smile. Patronizing, sure, but there's more to it than that.

"You tell me, Jack."

Tommy tries to save me by putting an arm around my

neck and saying, "Dude, love is the hard-on I get when I sit next to you," but Jess ignores him.

"Do you love Socrates?" she asks.

I look into those cross-eyed little eyes. Those eyes came from *me*. From *us*. I still can't quite believe it.

"Are you—are you absolutely sure he's mine?"

Jess lets out a long, "Woooooow. Are you really asking me that? *NOW?* I mean—*NOW?*"

"It's just that I—I want to hear it from you. For sure. For absolute sure."

She brushes a bit of hair out of her eyes. "It's all you, Jack. All twenty seconds."

It's Tommy's turn to snort liquid out of his nose.

"I think it was more like thirty," I say.

"Thirty's a good number," Homer says.

"It was twenty-six," Jess says. Another patronizing smile.

"Dude," Tommy says, turning sideways to face me with this real serious expression on his face. "How awesomely awkward would it be if I make a superhero joke *right now*? About Flash. And you. Done in a Flash. Like Flash. Jack? Jack?"

Whatever he sees in my face convinces him not to

pursue this avenue of conversation. "Fine, man," he says. "Go and ruin my fun." More silence. "Anyway, I don't see what's the big deal. So Jacky-boy got a little overexcited his first time—"

"Oh, it wasn't his first time," Jess says.

"So Jacky-boy got a little overexcited his second time—"

"Oh, it wasn't his second time."

"Well, okay, he was having an off day. Everyone is entitled to their—"

"Oh, it—"

"OKAY," I say, loud. "I think, that I need to go now. To the bathroom. Now." I stand. Hand Socrates off to Jess. "Good-bye."

"*Au revoir*, my darling," Jess says, and blows me a kiss.

"*Salaam Aleikum*," Homer says, forkful of pancake hovering by his mouth.

"*Gute Fahrt, mein Freund*," Tommy says, standing up to let me through. He blows me a kiss, too.

Did Tommy just tell me to have a good fart in German?

I say, "I will, don't you worry about me," flick the two of them off, clarify, "Not directed at you, Homer," and head for the bathroom.

From behind, Jess calls, "Sure, when I have half a minute to spare," and Tommy says, "Name a time and a place!"

The water from the sink courses over my hands. Crumpled paper towels lie scattered by the garbage can. I stoop down to throw them away, and my phone falls out of my pocket.

It flashes red.

I pick it up and find a bunch more messages from, yes, pretty much every single living member of my family.

Mom's last text is: *Please call.*

Sent at 11:47 A.M.

I sigh, real melodramatic. And then, I call her.

"Jack?" she says, before I have a chance to speak. She doesn't sound like she did before. She sounds tired.

"Yeah, Mom."

"Oh, Jack . . ."

"Mom," I say. "Please, just relax. Okay? I don't want you to freak out. Okay?"

"Okay, Jack. Can you just tell me why, Jack? I mean of all the things to do on your eighteenth birthday, kidnapping a baby—"

"He's my son, Mom." I hesitate. "Your grandson."

The lines goes quiet.

"My grandson?" she croaks.

"Yeah. Jess . . ." I stop. She doesn't know about Jess. "My ex-girlfriend," I say, "she wanted to give him away. And I couldn't. I had him in my hands and I couldn't."

"Oh, Jack," Mom says finally. "Why didn't you tell us? Me?"

"I don't know," I say. That's a lie, though. Telling them would have made it more real. I wanted to pretend it didn't happen. I'd been doing it so well I'd forgotten I was pretending at all—until yesterday morning.

"Can you—can you at least tell me if you're all right? You and him?"

"Yeah, Mom. We're all right."

"Where are you now?"

*In the bathroom of Pancake Palace, while Socrates, Homer, Socrates's mother, and my friend Tommy—you remember Tommy, right?—all wait outside for me to finish so we can go and steal a yacht.*

Instead, I say, *"Mom."*

"Jack, you know if something happens to him, even if it's not your fault . . ."

*"Mom."*

"Okay," she says. "Okay."

I hesitate. "Mom," I say. "What did you feel when you saw me the first time? After I was born?"

She exhales. "What I felt—"

"Mom, please. I need to know."

More silence.

"I need to know if it's normal that I don't know for sure if I love Socrates."

"You mean—your son?"

"Yeah."

"Oh, Jack . . ."

"Mom."

"Okay. Okay . . . Honestly, Jack. Honestly, I was delirious and in a lot of pain and I've always been ashamed, but at the time, at the time I didn't know what to feel. I was in so much pain and you were crying your head off—

"I'm sorry," she says.

"It's okay," I say. "So you didn't love me right away?"

"Jack, once I recovered a bit and took you in my arms and you weren't crying—that was really nice. I think I loved you then. It took me much longer to realize. Well"—she lets out a long breath—"it took me much longer to realize—to realize what it meant. Being a mother. It's killing me what you're doing. There's got to be a better way—"

"He's my son, Mom," I say. "My son." *And my friend.*
"I'm just trying to say good-bye. Once I give him up I
won't get to be a part of his life anymore. So I want to say
good-bye. Hello, good-bye."

"I always loved that song," she says.

"I know, Mom."

# 9

## Revolt Against the Fates, Infinity, the Typical Resolution of Quests, and Hallmark Cards

**S**houting from inside the restaurant. Can't make the words out. I edge the door open and my heart falls—a police officer at our table. Jess holds a crying Socrates, Homer's talking, gesticulating wildly, and I swear I hear him say, "We're all stardust here!"

This is it. This is how the story ends. In Pancake Palace. But then—the cop's alone. *Maybe if I run . . . If I get him to chase me, Tommy and Jess can get Socrates and*—but he sees me, half in and half out of the bathroom.

"There he is. There he is. All right, boy," he calls. "Come on out. Come over—"

He doesn't get to finish the sentence. Homer leaps out of the booth and tackles him with a roar. "Run," Homer yells, from the floor, on top of the cop, who's screaming, "THEY NEVER SHOW YOU THIS PART IN THOSE GODDAMN POLICE BRUTALITY VIDEOS!"

In the truck, Jess tries to buckle Socrates into his car seat, but her hands are shaking and the little guy is screaming at us with such fury you'd never believe he and I have intimate conversations about the nature of the universe and our place in it. Finally he's buckled but Tommy can't get the damn truck to start. Seconds pass. Jess keeps saying, "Oh shit, oh shit, oh shit," and I keep saying, "Come on, come on." Tommy says, "Never thought I'd say this but now I kind of wish I'd kept the Beemer." The front door of Pancake Palace bursts open and through it steps the cop. He pulls out a taser and yells, "Out of the truck, *now*!" Then the engine catches, and Tommy floors it.

Within minutes we're out of Harmony with the cop right behind us.

"Jack, program the damn GPS, will you? Get us to a highway."

I have no idea how to do that, because *oh yeah*, the goddamn menus are all in German. Jess has her eyes closed.

Her lips are moving, though, and if I didn't know any better I'd say she was praying. Socrates is still crying.

"Fucking hell," Tommy says, "can you two shut him up? I can't think."

"Trying," Jess says, and bends down to whisper into a red and quivering ear. She plants a kiss on his brow and strokes him gently on the cheek.

A sign for I-95. I almost cry from relief. At the merge, Tommy slows, brings us to an abrupt stop. The cop's still right behind. He gets out of his car, runs for us. Tommy throws a glance back and guns the engine. We leave the officer breathing our exhaust fumes.

Minutes later, Tommy takes the exit ramp to Pittsfield, yet another small town in a state of small towns, and this one doesn't even have a mythological name going for it.

I check the rearview every other second. We lost him. Tommy drives us down local streets. After a while Jess says, "I don't mean to sound critical of this wonderful dynamic duo thing you two have going on up there, but where the hell are we going? We've passed that McDonald's twice already."

"It's a Burger King, for Christ's sake," Tommy says.

"What?"

"He's right, Jess," I say, even though I have no idea what they're talking about. "It was a Burger King."

"Wow," is all Jess has to say in response.

"Cops probably got my license plate now, if they didn't already have it," Tommy says, voice distant. "We'll probably need another car or something."

"There are thousands of cars on the highway. We don't need another car. I told you this isn't *Grand Theft Auto*," Jess says.

"You got that right. In *Grand Theft Auto* there's no whiny tag-along . . ." He lets out a deep breath, and closes his eyes for just a second.

"Finish that thought, asshole," Jess says.

"TOMMY," I say, as the traffic light ahead turns red.

We rear-end a pink minivan and the airbags deploy with a POP. White dust flies everywhere. *Pain.* In my nose. Socrates is crying, *again*, but a quick look tells me he's fine.

"Oh, fuck me," Tommy says to the gray balloon trying to smother him. He looks like he just got mugged. By an inanimate object.

Jess: "Piece of shit seventeen-year-old goddamn drivers and their fucking road trips to grandma's house—it was a red fucking light—bright as day—like the seventh time you've almost *killed*—"

Tommy: "I didn't *see*—"

Jess: "Bright as the fucking day. Bright as the fucking sun. Bright as—"

Tommy: "Look. The sun is way brighter. Okay? *Okay?* The sun—"

Jess: "Barely got their driver's license, and now they think they can drive around stealing babies like Jason fucking Statham—"

Tommy: "You know what? Fuck Jason Statham. I already told you—and it's not even, wasn't even *vaguely* comparable to the sun. The sun is way brighter. The sun would burn out our retinas. Are my retinas burned out? Are *yours* burned out?"

Jess: "You wouldn't know a burnt-out retina if it bit you in the ass."

Tommy: "That doesn't, that doesn't even—"

The van we hit pulls over.

"Guys," I say, "I don't mean to interrupt your bonding moment, but maybe we should just leave. If the police come—"

"I'll handle it," Tommy says, and pulls us over behind

the van. He gets out of the truck. Jess and I exchange a look, then follow. Neither car is banged up too bad. *We should've just left.* The other driver's this high-school-age brunette with her hair up in a bun. She stomps toward us on four-inch platform heels. "That was my birthday present, jackass," she says.

Tommy smiles at her.

"I'll need your insurance and registration and we'll need to call the police," she says. "You look horrible by the way."

"You don't need to see my identification. The name's Tommy. And you don't need to call the cops. We aren't the guys you're looking for." Even though he's not looking at me, even though we're on the run and just crashed into some cheerleader who gets pink minivans for birthday presents, he goes and makes a *Star Wars* reference that he knows only I will get.

Total. Geek.

She squints at him. "Are you retarded?"

"You know, I get that question a lot," Tommy says. "I'm starting to think it's a new sort of come-on or something. And the funny thing is, coming from you, it kind of works." He winks at her. "How about we forget this whole insurance-registration-cop business and I take you out for a movie sometime?"

The brunette whips out her phone. "I'm calling Mommy," she says.

"Don't take this the wrong way, but I think it might be a little early for me to be meeting your parents—"

"And Mommy will call the cops."

I don't understand the logic involved in making Mommy the middleman. "Why not just call the cops?" I ask.

They both look at me like I've just *poofed* into existence, which is impossible, because I'm stardust and thus have always existed and will always exist.

"Who are you?" The way she says "you," it sounds like I belong in the same category as a slug. And hepatitis C. I take offense. As often happens when I'm insulted, I cannot think of what to say.

"Look," Tommy says, "if we're going to have a functional relationship, you're going to have to dial your hostility down a notch."

"Are you retarded?" she says again.

"Look," Tommy says, "you already got me to agree to a date. No need to backtrack. Now, I know you're probably a little upset at the whole bashed-in minivan business. And that's understandable. But instead of involving the cops here and parents and insurance companies and going through all that hassle, why don't you consider this an act of divine intervention and use it as an excuse to get rid of that ugly pink monstrosity?"

I know what's coming next.

"You are retarded, aren't you?" she says, now in a soft, sad voice.

"Only if you want me to be," Tommy says.

She punches three digits on her cell.

We scramble into the truck, Tommy gives the brunette a teary good-bye wave, and we drive off. She runs after us in her high heels, screaming.

"That went well," Jess says.

"Tommy has a way with the ladies," I say.

"Dude, I totally hit a home run," Tommy says. "I bet you a hundred bucks she Facebook friends me."

"Tommy, you wrecked her car and then drove off after hitting on her. I'm pretty sure she won't Facebook you."

"Jack," Jess says, "I think you're drastically overestimating the qualifying criteria of Facebook friendship."

"Right. I've accepted Facebook friends on the basis of

their having a pretty profile pic. Jack—this is where you compliment my profile pic," Tommy says.

"Dude, you have such a pretty profile pic," I say. "That's why I friended you in the first place."

"Exactly," he says. "Wait—*what?*"

"Yeah, man. I love your smile. But she still won't friend you. Do you know how many Tommys there are? If you had a less generic name, maybe you'd have a chance. And even if she did friend you, that's, like, not even first base. It's, like, walking onto the field."

"More like sitting in some nosebleed seat eating a ridiculously overpriced hotdog and watching other people walk onto the field," Jess says.

"More like eating a microwavable hotdog and watching other people walk onto the field on your ten-year-old piece-of-shit TV that has a dent in the top big enough to use as a cup holder," I say.

"If my girlfriend threw chairs at me I'd probably be hatin', too," Tommy says. "Besides, my TV is a plasma and Hebrew National make some good fucking hot dogs."

"Ex-girlfriend," Jess says. "And I prefer Oscar Mayer."

"Ex-girlfriend," Tommy says.

"They were more like tosses, really," I say.

• • •

Afternoon turns to evening, clouds clear away into a darkening blue. Along a cracked and bumpy forest road, we pass a car that ran into a tree. The police are there, and an ambulance. And a body. The boy's face is bloody, and he doesn't move. Then we've gone past them. Their lives, their ends fade away in the rearview mirror. I turn to Socrates and his eyes are sad.

"Tommy. Could you—pull over? I—uh—need a minute."

He throws me a concerned look. "Can you wait a few? I want to put some more miles between us and the police."

"Okay," I say, eyes on the window. Wildflowers and daisies line the road.

A little later, in the shadow of the forest, in the orange glow of a setting sun, I walk with Socrates along the shoulder.

How to start? How to begin?

"I know you're thinking about the boy. About the accident—*all* accidents. About *evil*. I guess, well, one kind of evil is when bad things happen to good people. And they do. Happen, I mean. What Epicurus said is, if there is evil in the world and God allows it, then either God endorses evil or he is powerless to stop it, and as such, isn't much of a God at all. It's easy to lose faith in a creator who made a world where a drunk driver can take the life of an entire family returning from a night out at the movies, where bombs exchanged by men in concrete bunkers fall on children playing in the streets."

*"So you want to live in a world without evil?"*

"Not just me. Everyone. The children being bombed, for starters. I'm sure they want a world without evil."

*"You believe yourself to be good, right?"*

". . . Well, yeah. I guess. But your adoptive parents aren't big fans of me at the moment. But what does that have to do with anything?"

*"My adopted parents. If they knew you, if they knew what you're trying to do—you think they'd see you as decent, right? As good?"*

"Yes, I guess."

*"And Tommy? Is he good? And Jess? She's good?"*

"Well—yes—but so what?"

*"So they're good but not perfect. They've hurt you, haven't they? And you, them? You've done evils to each other?"*

"Yes—we've hurt each other."

*"Well, that's just it, then. Would Tommy be Tommy if he*

*could never hurt you? Would Jess be Jess if she could never throw chairs at you? Would you be you if you hadn't made off with me? Your—no—our free will gives us choices and because we're not perfect, it's not always clear which choice is the right one . . . So yes, we can be wrong. Yes, the world's a messy place. But a world in which we always knew what was right and had no choice but to do it, that would be a world of puppets. A world without the possibility of* evil, *but also without the possibility of* Good, *because Good can't be automatic. It has to be chosen. What's more is, a world without the possibility of Good is a world without the possibility of us. A world without Tommy, Jess, you, or me."*

I have to shake my head and laugh at how *ballsy* he is. "Easy for you to say. You're not the children being bombed. This kind of argument—it's an argument from *privilege.* You're in a first-world country, you'll be brought up by some bourgeois engineer-accountant couple who'll vacation at ski resorts and golf resorts and give you falconry lessons. It's easy for *you* to say we're better off in a world where there's evil."

*"No. What I'm saying is we—none of us—would* exist *in a world without good and evil . . . Because we're not puppets."*

"If you're going to argue that evil is justified by our free will—"

"*No, what I'm saying is the* possibility *of evil is* necessary *if we are to have free will.*"

"Okay, fine. The possibility of evil is necessary for us to have free will. But you can't prove we actually have free will in the first place! You can't prove we're *not* puppets. Didn't we say before, in Troy, that what we do is determined by who we are, and who we are is shaped by the forces we can't control? Call them The Fates; call them biology, social conditioning, and environmental factors . . . Those are our strings, Socrates! Can you see them?"

"*Okay, Mr. Cynic. Tell me this. Why are you standing here?*"

"What?"

"*Why are we standing here, in a forest, near the edge of Maine talking about Epicurus and free will versus determinism? Weren't you the one who made Tommy stop the car so we could talk about the evil in the world? Jack, it doesn't matter if we* actually *have free will! It doesn't matter if there's* actually *Good and Evil!*"

"But—"

"*No buts! These are just more unanswerable questions. What matters is what* you *believe, because what you believe limits the universe. Remember? And if you don't believe in Good and Evil, then why are you standing here, going on*" *about children dying from bombs? Why are you so upset at an injured boy you never knew? If you really don't believe in free will, in good and evil, why not throw* me, *your* son, *why not throw your son into the next incoming car? Blame it on your lack of free will!"*

I say nothing. Then, "You're cheating. You're sidestepping the questions that matter. Again."

*"Why is the state of the universe more important than the state of* us? Of *you. Don't you get it, Jack? I'm not real. I'm two days old. I can't talk. I haven't even come to terms with my own existence, much less anyone else's. You're not arguing with me. You're arguing with yourself, about what* you *really believe in. So just be honest with yourself. What do you believe in? What do I believe in?"*

I hold Socrates up and he's only a baby. Not a philosopher. A baby who won't remember any of this. Any of our talks. Any of our journey.

It's like I just stuck my tongue in an electric socket.

This. *This* could be my ceiling to end all ceilings, this, my son and me standing here, together, trying to puzzle out the meaning of it all, with Jess and Tommy waiting in the car, all of us on our way to Grandma's house. To Grandma's house with Socrates.

*"So live. Live while you can and believe in right now. Believe in a trip to Grandma's house with your two best friends and your son."*

"It's just—it's just so hard to believe, when you doubt so much. We're all headed in different directions. Tommy, Jess, me, you, even Bob. Don't you see? How can I believe that *this* matters if it doesn't last?"

*"You can't have faith without doubt."*

"That doesn't even answer the question!"

My head's spinning as I return to the truck. I want very much to hug Tommy and Jess, to hold them tight.

I don't. I only say, "Sorry to keep you waiting."


An unimpressive-looking sign bids us "Welcome to Vermont." Our border crossing is pretty anticlimactic, as Vermont looks exactly like New Hampshire. The only difference is it's drizzling here. We pull off the road to wait the rain out. The world outside is one of those impressionist paintings that only makes sense if you keep far enough away.

We're not far enough away. How far enough away *is* far enough away? When astronauts go up into space and look down on earth from the international space station, do they see it clearly?

Is that far enough away?

The storm pounds our truck. When I was a kid, I would run outside after a storm to breathe in the wet air and splash in the puddles. Bob would always scold me, saying I'd catch a cold, but she would always be smiling as she did it, like maybe deep down she wished she could have gone out and jumped in the puddles with me.

"So," Tommy says.

"So," I say.

Jess doesn't say anything.

"Jess," I say. "You were supposed to say 'so.'"

"What—oh, sorry."

She's in the back, focused on Socrates. He's asleep in his car seat and she's humming a melody softly to him.

"You okay?" I say.

She breaks it off. "Yeah, Jack. I mean. I'm tired. All considering, I could be worse. I guess. Hypothetically, any-way." She smiles weakly.

"That's the spirit," Tommy says. "Just think—at least a meteor isn't going to hit the earth and destroy all life."

"Does that help you, Tommy?" she asks.

"Nah," Tommy says. "Usually I imagine meteors hit-ting specific people. I've got no beef with the earth."

"I was thinking," Jess says. "About something you said."

"Me?" Tommy asks.

"Yeah. You said . . ." Her lips twitch. "You said if you were going to have a baby your parents would be there. Maybe—maybe I made a mistake. Maybe I should've told my parents."

That comes as a surprise to me. "But how—"

"Why should they?" she says in a tired voice. "I didn't go home for the summer. Haven't been home for a year now. It's my business, isn't it? My decision?"

"Would they have wanted you to keep him?"

She shakes her head. "No. They probably would have told me . . ." She pauses. "They would have told me what you did, Jack. They would have said I wasn't ready. That neither of us was ready. That it wouldn't be responsible to bring a child into the world when I know I can't give it what it needs. That I needed to focus on school and internships. Having a career after college. All that other bullshit." She plays with a bit of her hair, wrapping it round and round her finger. "I just didn't want to deal with them. They're in Hawaii, you know. My parents, I mean. But I was exaggerating when I said everyone I knew was drunk, on vacation, or dead. The truth is, Jack, you were the one I wanted there most, despite—" She sighs. "But then you got there and I couldn't help feeling so bitter. So—I don't know."

"I'm glad you called me, Jess."

"Yeah. Me too."

"Me three," Tommy says, completely ruining the mood.

The rain continues to fall.


The night air rushes in through the cracked window. I stare at the GPS screen, half-asleep. We just passed this place called Jeffersonville and it says we're about a half hour east of St. Albans. From somewhere far away, Socrates is crying.

The clock at the bottom of the screen says it's 11:30 P.M. Feels later than that.

"Hey, Tommy, will you pull over? I think—Socrates needs a change."

"Sure," he says, sounding tired.

I bring the little guy up to the front with me to check his diaper. Clean. Jess is sleeping, stretched out in this weird, diagonal sort of way. She stirs, but I whisper, "I've got it. Go back to sleep.

"I'm going to get some formula from the back," I say to Tommy.

"I'll help you."

Tommy opens the cab and hands me a carton from the cooler. I fill Socrates's bottle, spilling some formula onto the pavement. We listen to him gulp it down. The moon is bright, and our journey, *unreal.*

"It's—crazy. What we're doing is crazy. To Grandma's house with Socrates."

"Yeah, man," he says. "You know, man. I've—I've been thinking about what you said before. And I kind of don't want this to end. I might have even got us a little lost on purpose. A few times."

Why would he—*how* could he—with a GPS three inches from his face . . .

"Like, you know how in all those movies where people blow shit up and then it all gets resolved in the end?" he asks. "Or, like, when a bunch of midgets and dwarfs and effeminate elves go on some heroic quest and do hero things and then defeat evil stuff and bring peace and love and fairies back to the land?"

"Fairies?"

"Fairies, man. The fucking fairies."

"Yeah. Fucking fairies."

"I know you want the fairies and the love and the peace, I know that's why we're doing this, man," he says. "That's why they always do it. Because the evil stuff wants to eat the fairies and enslave the proletariat and commodify love."

High school psychology taught me it's important to give out verbal cues when someone else is talking, even when you have no idea what they're talking about. My verbal cue is "Yeah. Fuck Hallmark cards. And their commodification of love."

"Fucking Hallmark cards," Tommy says. "But the thing is, what they don't show you is after. What do you do after? After evil is defeated and peace and love and fairies are brought back to the land? What do the heroes do if they have no quest to go on?"

"I suppose they settle down," I say.

"Yeah, man, but do you realize what that means?" There's something desperate in his voice, something I don't think I've ever heard before. "Settling down is just like you said it was. Settling down means growing old and getting jobs and being productive fucking members of society, and most of all it means drifting apart, like the ants on the pentagons and the glass in the wind and shit. What keeps the heroes together if not their fight to unite the workers of the world against their fairy-eating overlords?"

"Dude, my brain's a little fuzzy right now, but this is an extended metaphor, right?"

Tommy looks at me a long time. "Well, kind of. But it's also like, you've seen *Star Wars* and *Lord of the Rings* and *Narnia* and *Harry* Frickin' *Potter.* You've seen at the end how everyone is always so happy. And that's the part they show you. How everyone's so happy. They don't show you ten years later."

"Actually, I believe *Harry* Frickin' *Potter*—"

"Well, okay, in that case, I wish I hadn't seen ten years later."

Tommy has a point. What do you *do* after you've got your Golden Fleece? *What then?* After all those thousands of words about Harry and friends fighting Voldemort, what are Harry and company left with in the wake of old Voldy's defeat? Typical, middle-class lifestyles. Their quest is done. Finished. Kaput. Now, instead of a quest, they have nine-to-five jobs. Instead of a journey, they have the everyday Floo Network commute. And they have kids but it's, like, to the kids, to Severus Albus Lupin Dumbledore Frickin' Potter, Harry Potter's just Dad. And is that enough for

Harry Frickin' Potter? Is it enough to be just Dad, like a billion other just-dads out there in the world?

I hold Socrates a little tighter.

Well sure, Harry Potter is just Dad. And sure, I'm just Dad, too. Unlike the billion other just-dads though, I'm just Dad to Socrates, just a friend to Tommy and Jess, just a grandson to Bob. Nobody else can say that. Except, well, I will never really get to be just Dad to Socrates. And if I lose Tommy and Jess and my grandma, which I probably will, there's so many hexagons and the soccer ball is spinning and *oh*—the hurricane winds! If I lose them all, then Jess would have had it right back there in the hospital, what a brilliant instance of foreshadowing that would have been on the Fates' part. Maybe all I'm destined to be is *just* Jack.

"You okay there, man?" he asks.

"I'll never get to be just Dad for him," I say.

Tommy sighs. "I know, man. I'm sorry." He sits down on the pavement, hands on his knees, and looks up at the sky. This is the closest we'll ever be. This is our escape. Our secret closet, our letter of invitation to Hogwarts, our death-star run. After this we're back to the real world, and from there the hill slopes down and only stops at six feet under.

"It's your fucking fault," I say. "We were at the same goddamn high school and you went and dropped out. And then we could've gone to the same college, but you went and enlisted instead."

"My dad," he starts. "My dad—he, like, had my whole life planned for me. He had me going to the same private school he went to and after that he wanted me to go to Cornell. Hell, man, he had my *major* picked out for me. I was trying to run away from *him*, Jack. From all his *plans*. Not from—you know."

"So. So you feel free now, then?"

He sighs again. "No. I don't know, Jack. Sort of. I don't know. You want to know the funniest part? The real kicker?"

"Go for it."

"A week after I told him I was going to enlist, he comes into my room and tells me to do whatever I want. Just don't go into the army. That's all I really wanted—a chance to decide for myself. And yet, now that I *could* do anything I wanted, I had no direction. Like, think about it. What would you do if you weren't going to college next year?"

"No idea."

"Right?"

"No idea at all."

"It's scary. Knowing you can do anything is the same as not knowing what the fuck to do. Right? So I enlisted anyway."

When I don't respond, he says, "You know, you could enlist, too." We both know this is a joke. I don't think I even fit the minimum weight requirement.

My anger ebbs out of me. "Maybe we'll get to be cell-mates in jail," I say.

"Ha. That would be fun. Almost as good as being roommates in college. Though I daresay the hookup scene will probably leave something to be desired."

"My dick is shriveling up at the thought."

"Anti-boner," he says.

"Anti-boner," I say. I play back Tommy's words in my head, over and over again, trying to make sense of them. Just when I'm ready to give up, Socrates whispers, *"Remember old Zeno!"* in my ear. But what does Zeno have to do with fairies and effeminate elves and Hallmark cards and quests?

Then it clicks. I am filled with a sense of awe.

Journeys, quests, they both end and don't end, they have to end and can't end. What Zeno said was, okay, to move a given distance, one must first move half of that given distance. So if you have a chicken crossing a road, before the chicken can cross the road, it must first cross half the road. But before the chicken can cross half the road, it must first cross a quarter of the road. And before the chicken can cross a quarter of the road, it must first cross an eighth. Before an eighth, a sixteenth. And on and on and on, to infinity, because there is no "smallest" number, and *because* there is no smallest number, any given number can be broken down an infinite number of times—which means, *which means* there is infinity in any given distance, any number, and yes—*any span of time.* Yet here's the most remarkable thing—the chicken does appear to cross the road.

How does the chicken cross the road, when in so doing it might as well be traversing the whole damn universe? How will we ever reach Grandma's house going seventy-three or however many miles per hour through the dark, when her house might as well be a star shining a hundred light-years away? How does a second pass when that second contains in itself, all of time? Maybe the second does not pass at all, maybe the chicken does not cross the road at all, but then, where would that leave us? Could the second both pass and not pass, the chicken cross and not cross, could you both get a hold of the Golden Fleece and waste your whole life searching for it? Could you lose and not lose, age and not age, die and not die? Maybe it's like with Schrödinger's cat, the universe splits and in one there is the passing and in another there is a keeping and somehow these are tied inextricably together.

"Tommy," I say.

"Yeah?"

"I kind of want to scream."

"Why?"

"Because. Because did you know that when a chicken crosses a road, it might as well be crossing the whole universe?"

"No, Jack. I did not, in fact."

"It wants to get to the other side, 'cause that's where the Golden Fleece is, but how can it ever get there?"

"But, Jack," Tommy says. "What would a chicken want with a fleece?"

"It's not about the fleece, Tommy. It's about crossing the road to get to the fleece." So I explain it to him. I explain what Zeno discovered and he says, "Weird."

"Yeah," I say.

"You know, it kind of makes me believe," Tommy says. "In magic. And quests. And fairies. And Harry Frickin' Potter. And staying young forever. And growing old. Chickens running after golden fleeces, even. I don't know."

"It makes me want to scream."

"It makes me want to take an aspirin." He massages his temples.

"Headache?"

"Yeah."

"Because life doesn't make sense," I say. My voice is high—almost giddy, from weariness and excitement, frustration and the tiniest feeling of the sublime, of grasping and missing and grasping and missing. It's like Socrates said, some questions will never be answered . . .

"Yeah," he says. "No fucking sense."

"It doesn't make any fucking sense," I say, voice still high, still giddy. Tommy winces. "The most basic things of all, numbers, dimensions, length, time, none of it makes sense. But we're here, aren't we? Right? We're here, driving to my fucking grandma's house." I laugh. I can't help it. "We're going about our lives like they're ordinary, but they're not! They're not. They're so extraordinary we can't even begin to understand them! It makes me think of this book, this book *Never Let Me Go* by this Japanese guy, Ishiguro. A character"—I pause— "he's one of the main characters, Tommy, there's this scene near the end where he gets out of the car and goes out into a field and just *screams* at it all, at life and death and the futility of dreams and hopes and shit and not understanding, living in a universe he can't understand and why it all happens the way it does, why the Fates shape everything the way they do. Sometimes I want to do what he did. Let loose."

"You—want to do it?" Tommy says.

"What?"

"Just scream," Tommy says. "Like the Tommy in the book."

"Now?"

"Yeah," he says.

"Yeah," I say.

We go out a ways, into a field. The grass rises up to our knees and hisses softly in the wind. We look at each other, all three of us. Tommy grins sheepishly, as if to say, "You go first."

I go first. I open my mouth and scream—have the urge

to close my eyes while I do it. I fight it, I keep them open and look up, up, and soon Tommy's voice joins mine. We're on our knees, hollering at the universe, *limiting* it—is this why wolves howl at the moon?—when Socrates joins in, too.

# 10

## Crossing the Seas (okay, so it's a lake) in *The Pequod*

**M**oonlight illuminates the still waters of St. Albans Bay. The marina is small and dimly lit, mostly deserted, with only a handful of ships tied up at dock. Tommy's father's yacht is by far the most impressive boat, at least three times the size of any of the others. The name painted in great, bold letters along the side reads *The Pequod*. I have Socrates in my arms—quiet for the moment—his basket slung over my shoulder in a rather awkward fashion. I'm rocking back and forth to keep the little guy happy. He gets cranky every time I stop.

"Oh, loosen up, will you?" Tommy says in a not-very-loose voice, probably due to the weight of the cooler in his hands. What a drama queen. There's only a bit of formula in there. And of course, the ice. And granted, the cooler's pretty big.

"You sure you don't want us to help you with that? And by us, I mean Jack," Jess says. "If you hurt yourself I don't think he'll be able to live with himself."

"And you?" he asks.

"Oh," Jess says, with a wave of the hand, "I'll be fine."

"Seriously though, Tommy—" I say.

"Jack." He grunts, shifts the weight of the cooler. "Don't be an idiot."

"But I won't be able to live with myself—"

"Get a divorce. That's why I did. Now me, myself, and I are all very much separate and happy with a capital H." Now come on."

After we clamber onto the deck of the *The Pequod*, Tommy leads us into the cabin, which is decorated precisely the way he hates. Floor-to-ceiling bookshelves line the walls. Dante, Virgil, and my old friend Homer. Could his dad be any more pretentious? I mean really? *Homer?*

An elevated white-leather sofa encircles the wheel and captain's chair, beyond which lie the controls and several sleek flat-screen monitors. An expensive-looking rug covers the floor, depicting a scene from, I think, *Moby-Dick*. The jaws of the great white whale rise out of the stormy ocean to swallow a ship so small by comparison it looks like a toy. His dad even got the ceiling painted—another image from *Moby-Dick*; in this one, there's a man standing alone in a lifeboat, struggling to hold a harpoon steady as waves crash around him. Only the tail of the whale is seen. It's a very big tail.

Tommy sets the cooler down with a grunt, and says, "Jack, put Socrates down and come here."

I comply, but warily. I hand Socrates to Jess and walk over to where he's standing by the wheel.

"I'm going to start this baby," he says, giving me a meaningful look. "I need to cast us off. All you need to do is hold on to the wheel and make sure we don't hit anything."

"Tommy, it has just occurred to me that this might not be the best idea."

"Which part?" Jess says. "Though I suppose it doesn't really matter. That train left a while ago," she says into Socrates's ear, but loud enough for us to hear.

"Here we go again," I say.

"We'll be fine, man," Tommy says. "I believe in you."

"But what if I hit an iceberg?" I say. "Or that little boat over there?"

"Dude, there totally aren't any icebergs floating around at this time of the year. I think. Besides. What kind of an idiot hits something that big?"

Ummm, the captain of the *Titanic,* for starters.

"And as for the little boat," he continues. "It won't be any great loss. I think I know the owner. He's a dick."

"I'll have you know," I say to Jess, "that if we do sink, I have no intention whatsoever of drowning for you. Some people would say pulling a Leonardo DiCaprio is romantic, but they're not the ones with their heads in the hypothetical water. If we drown, we should drown together."

"Agreed," Jess says. "If I hypothetically drown, I'm going to make damn sure you're hypothetically coming with me."

"Now that we've got that settled," Tommy says, "let's go!" He sticks the key in the ignition. The engine grumbles. He presses a few buttons in quick succession. "Be right back," he says, and runs off, to do whatever casting us off entails doing. I'm holding the wheel harder than I've held anything in my life, knuckles white, sweating with anticipation.

Must not hit the other boats. Or icebergs.

And then . . . the floor lurches under my feet.

We're moving, cutting through the water, but somehow our orientation is all wrong. We're angled at the dock. I turn the wheel, fast. Jess yells, "JACK!" and I yell, "JESS!" and we hear a *crack*, the yacht shudders, a few books fall from the bookcase, I nearly fall, but we're still going, except now there's the smaller boat looming up on us, moored and bobbing up and down in the water, and I'm frozen, all I can think is no big deal, Tommy thinks he remembers that the owner might be a dick so it's all good!

"JACK WHAT ARE YOU DOING?" Jess yells.

"I DON'T KNOW—"

Tommy scrambles into the cabin, eyes wide. *"TURN,"* he hollers, and that jolts me back. I turn. Close my eyes and turn the wheel.

Brace for impact.

Seconds pass.

I hear Tommy let out a deep breath. "Christ, Jack. *Christ,* that's the last time we're stealing my dad's yacht together." He takes the wheel from me with slightly shaking hands, slumps heavily into the captain's seat, and steers us out into the lake.

"We're not going to sink are we?" I ask, quiet.

"I think you just nicked the dock," he answers, also quiet. Eventually he sets the engine to neutral. Mumbles something—I could swear he says he needs to find *the manual*, but I'm doing my best to disbelieve my ears. He checks a closet in the corner of the cabin, and becomes engaged in furious battle with its inanimate residents. A mop launches a surprise attack. Tommy catches it. "Well fuck you, too," he tells it, and throws it back in disgust.

"Your dad did teach you to pilot this thing, didn't he?" Jess asks, and holds Socrates tighter.

"Yeah," Tommy says, still focused on the closet.

"So what do you need a manual for then? Are you sure you—"

"Look, I know how to pilot the damn boat, okay? It's just I nearly had a heart attack—"

"Sorry," I say sheepishly.

He glances in my direction briefly. "It's okay, Jack. What's a heart attack or two? Anyway the manual makes me feel more comfortable. All right? We used to go sailing out on Lake Champlain all the time when

I was a kid. Dad always said it was good to have the manual on hand. Anyway, I can't find it." He throws up his hands as if to say, *I tried.* He shuts the closet door and approaches the controls, frowning. "Maybe it's below deck. I mean I don't really need it." He doesn't sound convinced though.

"You know, it's not too late to go back to the car. It won't take that much longer," I say.

"Nah, we can't go back," Tommy says. "I aim to do Father proud."

"Isn't this is all so poetic?" Jess asks, looking at Socrates. "One father kidnapping his son for love and a son stealing his father's yacht out of a yearning for acceptance. I think I feel a tear coming on."

I lean forward to get a better look. "Oh, I don't think that's a tear," I say. "I think you're melting."

We head, with a hum, toward the moon's reflection in the lake. A monitor displays a map of Lake Champlain, with a purple line running northeast to southwest indicating our course from St. Albans to Clifford.

"Not so hard," Tommy says, wheel in his hands. He's in the captain's chair, Jess and I on the sofa, with Socrates in his basket right next to us. I've never sat on a more comfortable sofa in my life.

"It's like I remember," Tommy's saying. "Like driving a car. A really, really, really big car. On water."

"So nothing like driving a car?" I say.

"Exactly, man. You always know what I'm getting at. The computer says we should be there by dawn, barring any run-ins with icebergs, or, you know, *docks*, so you might as well make yourselves comfortable." In a slightly panicked voice, he adds, "*Here*, I mean. Make yourselves comfortable *here*. You guys can't leave me alone. I'll get bored. And lonely. And bored. The chances of me running into an iceberg rise in direct proportion to my loneliness and boredom."

"Better you than Jack I guess, but you don't actually think we'd trust you enough to leave you here alone?" Jess says. "You nearly got us killed half a dozen times in that truck of yours. And then the poodle you almost ran over—"

"There was a poodle?" I ask.

"Yeah, Jack," she says, "but you were too busy talking to Socrates about Aristotle to notice. Your BFF here almost turned the poor thing into roadkill."

"That poodle," Tommy says, "was jaywalking."

Socrates gurgles in agreement.

A few minutes later Tommy turns to me and says, "You know, I'd actually feel better if I had the manual. Just in case. You know?"

I *don't* know. But if the damn thing means that much to him . . . "I can try and find it—where do boat manuals typically reside?"

"Typically, in the cabin. This is a decidedly—*untypical?* Atypical? Untypical. A decidedly untypical situation, this is. It's probably below deck. That's like the only other place."

"I'll help you look," Jess says to me.

"Didn't you two just tell me you wouldn't leave me alone?" Tommy asks.

"As much as I don't want to leave you alone, I want you to drive us without some kind of higher form of guidance even less," Jess says.

"And since none of us are on particularly good terms with God, we figure a manual will have to do the job," I say.

"Well thanks, *Jack,* for that clarification. And here I thought you believed in me."

"I do. But as a great man whose name I can't remember once said, 'hope for the best, brace for the worst,' am I right?"

"Surprisingly, yes," Jess says.

"Statistically, it had to happen sooner or later," I say.

"Monkeys on typewriters and all," Tommy says.

"*Hey*," I say.

Tommy shrugs. "Statistics man!"

"We won't be long," Jess says.

I nod at Socrates's basket. "Just look after him for a bit."

"Sure man. Don't do anything fun without me!"

Below deck, Jess and I scour the living-room-kitchen-lounge area, searching in cabinets, in desks, on tables, beneath tables. Everywhere, framed pictures of Tommy smile at us from the walls. We find the manual in a closet, in a box, along with lifejackets, an inflatable raft, and a whistle. I grab the whole box. Just in case. You know. We're about to go back up, when, *yes*—staring back at me from a glass cabinet above the refrigerator—a bottle of alcohol. Commence internal struggle of mythic proportions.

*Devil: What are you waiting for, Jack? In a few hours you're going to get to Bob's house only to find that she thinks you're the milkman.*

*Angel: Don't listen—*

*Devil: You'll have to give up your son and you'll never see him again.*

*Angel: Now hold on—*

*Devil: This whole little "quest" of yours won't have meant shit, because Bob will be like "Why is the milkman showing me his baby?" and Socrates will be like "_____" because he's a newborn, you fucking* idiot.

*Angel: Now you just wait one gosh darn second.*

*Devil: What?*

*Angel: In calling* him *an idiot, you're calling both of* us *idiots, because we're an oversimplified imaginary personification of Jack's internal crisis that will inevitably end in you triumphing over me, because that's what always happens in the cartoons.*

*Devil: I wasn't talking about all of Jack. Just your half.*

*Angel: : o*

*Devil: Ahem. And by the way, Jack? Tommy and Jess? You'll never see them again. They don't even* like *you. Because you're craaaaazy. Case in point:* this. *And as for Bob? She'll get hit by a tractor-trailer next time she's taking a walk.*

"What are you looking at?" Jess says. She follows my gaze. "You're not seriously—"

But I am. "Just a swig or two," I say. I throw the bottle

in the box, and start back up to the cabin. "You're not allowed any. Doctor's orders."

"Excuse me?"

"Back, I see," Tommy says upon our return. "With a box." He has Socrates in one arm and the wheel in the other.

I deposit the box on the ground, grab the manual. He trades me Socrates for it.

"Thanks, mate. Knew I could count on you. Took you guys a while, though. You didn't do anything naughty without me, did you?"

"Oh, you have no idea," Jess says.

"Yeah, neither do I," I say, setting Socrates back in his basket.

"Wait," Tommy says, squinting into the box. "Is that—"

"Yep," Jess says.

"Yep," I say. "Cheers!" I raise the bottle to my mouth to take a nice, long sip, but Jess manhandles it out of my grasp.

"What are you doing?" I say.

"Yeah," Tommy says. "I'm pretty sure you're not supposed to—"

"Tommy. Jack. Are you lactating?"

Not last time I checked. I don't say this aloud, though.

Jess isn't joking. It's a serious question. She really wants to know if we're lactating.

"Does the simple act of peeing feel like breathing fire out of your vagina?"

I've never breathed fire out of a vagina, mine or otherwise, so I have no basis for comparison.

"Are you going to be giving up the kid that you spent nine months carrying around inside you tomorrow? And I suppose neither of you have an ex-boyfriend who almost capsized a boat and drowned you and said baby. *No?* Okay then. I'm glad we're in agreement that if there's anyone of us here who needs to kill a few brain cells, it's me." She throws a glance at Socrates before looking away.

Wow. Jess is going through just as much if not more than I am (including almost drowning), and she's *been* going through it all for the *past nine months.*

And I'm only realizing this now.

I am literally a jackass.

Within the hour all three of us are drunk and Socrates is like "*My dad is an* idiot" and "*OMG I am going to die.*" I change his diaper even though it's clean. Tommy's still at the wheel, Jess and me on the sofa, and I never want to leave. Ever. Also, the floor moves up and down and up and down, which would make leaving hard. If I was crazy enough to want to leave. Which I'm not.

"You know," Tommy says. And doesn't continue.

"Yeah," Jess says, cradling the tequila. She squints at it and says, "It's half empty. You guys already drank half of it. I can't believe I let you—"

"Let me?" Tommy says, indignant. "It's my fucking alcohol."

"Oh, go steal a yacht," Jess says with a wave of her hand.

"Maybe I will," Tommy says. "Maybe—Jack, can you believe this?"

I don't know what to believe. I caught my reflection in the glass a few minutes ago and I was like, *wow,* those things are big. (By things I mean ears. My ears.) And not *just* big. Big big. Dumbo big. Flappy-flappy big. I open my mouth to consult Tommy and Jess, but stop myself. The last thing I need is for them to commiserate with me on the flappiness of my ears.

"Jack," Tommy says, louder.

"What?"

"I don't know, man."

"Tommy?" I say.

"Yeah, man."

I take the plunge. "Do I have big ears?"

"The biggest, man. The absolute biggest, and don't let anyone tell you different."

"I—I never noticed how big they were."

"Dude," he says, leaning on the wheel for support, "I love your fucking ears. Keep 'em."

"I don't know," Jess says, and tilts her head. "They're kind of—"

"Kind of what?" I say.

"They kind of—well—stick out a bit. They're kind of stick-outy, you know?"

"I know." Never have I meant anything more than I mean those two words now.

"So what if they're stick-outy?" Tommy says. "Jack. Listen to me." He snaps his fingers without making the snappy noise. "Listen to me, man. There are people who would kill for your ears. Kill."

"But they are a little stick-outy," Jess says.

I look past Tommy then, through the glass to the dark sky beyond. Picture the dark seas. And icebergs hiding beneath dark waves.

"Tommy," I say.

"Yeah, man."

"Are you sure you're okay? To pilot the ship."

"Oh, man, the ship—she's fine. She's fine. Like an arrow. You point her and she flies like an arrow." He pats the wheel to show me how fine everything is.

"Ships don't fly," Jess points out rather astutely.

"No," Tommy frowns. "They don't."

We puzzle over that for a moment. Tommy's frown proves contagious. Soon we're not just drunks, but very serious drunks. Socrates is still like, "*My dad is an* idiot" and "*OMG I am going to die.*" I'm like, "*Chillax son. Everything is O.K.*"

"Jack," Tommy says. "I don't think I can do it."

"What do you mean you don't think you—what are we talking about?" Jess says.

"If the ship's not an arrow, then I don't think I can pilot it," Tommy says.

"Tommy," I say. "You don't need to pilot an arrow."

"But that's just my point," Tommy says. "The ship is not an arrow."

"Actually," Jess says, "that was my point. But so what? Let the ship be whatever she wants to be. Why do you get to tell her about her being an arrow? Maybe she doesn't want to be your arrow. Maybe she doesn't want to fit neatly into your bow-and-arrow paradigm, your archery-based view of the world."

"But that's what I'm saying. If the ship's not an arrow, then someone needs to pilot her, but I can't pilot her."

"What do you mean you can't pilot her," Jess says. "You're piloting just fine."

"Yeah," I say. "Tommy, if you could only see how good you're piloting. If you could only see. Like in third person."

Tommy sighs and says, "Guys, you just don't get it. I've forgotten."

"Forgotten," I say.

"What do you mean you've forgotten?" Jess says. "You're doing it right now. You're doing it."

"Doing what?" Tommy says, throwing his hands up in the air. "I don't know what I'm doing! It's been too long. Dad hasn't taken me sailing in years. I've forgotten it all! If we die, it's going to be all his fault."

"Die?" Jess says, voice high. "What do you mean, die?"

"I mean," Tommy says, "hit an iceberg and drown. To death. We're going to drown to death."

"Tommy," I say, "you said there weren't any icebergs

this time of year. And I just told Socrates everything—"

"I lied, Jack. I lied. The icebergs are everywhere."

"Oh, enough of the icebergs," Jess says, grabbing the manual from where we left it. "Okay," she says. "We'll just read you the instructions and you keep piloting."

I nod in agreement, and lean in to get a better look at the table of contents. Item number one reads, "How to use the manual."

"Tommy," I say. "The manual is self-reflective."

"The best of them are, Jack. The best of them are," he says.

"Well, I think we should start from the beginning. The very beginning," Jess says. "If you're going to remember how not to get us drowned that's the place to start."

"I'm not going to have you read me a manual about reading a manual," Tommy says, pressing some buttons whose function I wouldn't be able to guess at even if I were sober. "Just look how long it is! We'll definitely be drowned before we even get halfway through."

The manual *is* rather thick.

"I agree with Tommy. I mean, just think about it. If you need a manual to read a manual, then maybe you need a manual to read a manual that tells you how to read the manual you really want to read? And where does it end? Where do the manuals end? They just keep going, guys. They keep going. It's an infinite regress. Just like with God and the universe and the soccer balls and hurricane winds and ceilings, for Christ's sake. Oh *God*, it's just like with the ceilings! You know? Guys? Guys?"

"Jack," Tommy says, "I love you, but sometimes I feel like slapping you."

"Jack," Jess says. Blinks. Squints. And redefines what it means to projectile vomit.

We race below deck, barely reaching the toilet in time for the second coming. I set Socrates and his basket on the tile floor (*Why did I bring him in the first place?*) and he observes the situation with a measure of puzzlement. *"Is this what adults do?"* he asks. But how should I know? I'm just a kid. Just a kid, just a drunk, just a drunk kid talking to Socrates while holding my ex-girlfriend's hair back as she pukes out a lung.

Jess washes her face, rinses her mouth. I hand her a paper towel. She gives me a quick peck, on the cheek. She's wet, still smells a bit like puke. And she missed a spot. Just under her chin. I can't look away. That's when I puke. The bathroom looks like someone went to take a crap and blew up instead.

*At least Socrates is untouched*—but the rising feeling comes again. I dive for the toilet and vomit up—yes, I'm pretty sure that's *my* lung. Once the business of my throwing up is done, I wash *my* face, rinse *my* mouth. Jess hands me a paper towel. I kiss her, on the lips, but she pushes me back.

"Don't get any ideas, Jack. Just gave birth, remember? Lactating, remember? Fire-breathing vagina, remember?"

"Yeah yeah, I remember, I remember."

"I think—I need to lie down for a while. I don't feel so great."

I take her by the hand, and lead her stumbling through the dark. I fumble along the walls for a light switch. Do not find it. Jess lets out a yelp. We trip and land on something furry. Maybe a bear. She's beside me. Laughing. We're lying on something that might be a bear and if she keeps laughing it might eat us. I want to stay there, beside her, and listen to her laugh. Even if that means getting eaten by a bear.

"Jess," I whisper.

"Yeah, Jack?"

"I think I loved you."

Her hand touches my face. "I think I loved you, too."

"Do you think we can get it back?"

"I don't know, Jack."

Socrates cries out from the bathroom.

"*Shit*," I say. We forgot him. I need to go to him. It's hard to get up, though. Jess and I—here and now, this is important, too, and if we don't have this talk *now*, we may never have it. Jess starts to rise, but I say, "I'll go."

I pick up Socrates and put him in the bathtub to check his diaper. Still clean. Three hours without a crap? Must be a record. Dude's probably hungry, that's why, so I press him to my chest with one arm, and with the other outstretched, I walk slow, out of the bathroom and into the dark.

"He's hungry," I say to Jess, somewhere unseen. "Where did we leave the cooler?"

Nothing. Then, "With Tommy, I think. In the cabin."

I pace myself. Real careful. Up the steps. One by one. Hand on the railing. Little by little.

The deck rocks beneath my feet and the stars shine overhead. Wind hits me hard. Spray from the lake peppers me like a dozen freezing fingers. I soak it in. Behind us is the coast of Vermont, where I left drinking beer from Solo cups with Jess and playing GoldenEye with Tommy. And the lights ahead?

I point at them, to show Socrates.

The lights ahead, growing closer, are the lights of New York. The lights of *Troy*.

Tommy, slumped over the wheel in just his underwear, grins at me knowingly when I stride through the door.

"Looking good, Jacky-boy," he says. "Looking. Good."

I should maybe say something nice about him, too. I go for, "You're really handling that wheel well."

"I try, man. I try."

I find Socrates's bottle in the cooler. Fill it up. He drinks a bit, then decides no, he'd rather cry.

"I'll be right back," I say to Tommy, and take Socrates outside again, let the wind swallow up his cries. He quiets down some, as if he's in awe at the vastness of the world and the cosmos gleaming above.

"At first, they thought the world was made of water." I hold Socrates up, over my head, so he can see.

"That everything was made from water, I mean." Who is *they*? Can't remember. Some Greek dude, probably. Definitely not a Roman. All the Romans did was copy the Greeks and build lots of roads.

"It kinda makes sense, right? Water falls down as rain. Gets soaked up by the ground. In the mornings, there's dew. You live on the coast or sail in a ship and you look about and there's water as far as you can see. You don't know about the whole water cycle yet. But then another guy comes along. Not a Roman. And this other guy, this different guy said, *no*, the world's made from air. He said stars are made from fire, and that's just really, really thin air. And then there's water, which is thick air. And rock, which is really, really thick air. But that's silly. So then a *third* dude, he said the source of all things is the unlimited."

The little guy falls silent. He's *listening*.

"But," I say. "The dude didn't know how the unlimited would turn into or bring about everything we know, right? 'Cause everything we know is limited. So what he did was, he said *a part* of the unlimited separated from the unlimited, and that *part* made all the stuff of our world."

I pause for effect. "Which is silly. Because for a part to separate from the unlimited means it was once part of the unlimited, was once unlimited itself, and how can the unlimited be separated into pieces? Wouldn't the pieces of the unlimited be unlimited? It doesn't solve the problem at all."

"*Maybe the pieces of the unlimited are unlimited? Do you know about set theory?*"

"From Buddhism to Calculus? And here I thought I was the drunk one—"

"*Shut up and listen. Do you know about set theory?*"

"Not really—"

"*Set theory teaches us some infinities are bigger than others. The set of all real numbers is bigger than the set of all even numbers, even though both are infinite. Think about Zeno's paradox. A road ten feet wide contains an infinity in itself, and yet we cross it anyway. Our infinity is bigger than the road's infinity. We traverse infinity, we limit infinity—that is what we do. Think about time. Time has to be infinite, because since time contains all change, if time were to have a beginning, there would be no accounting for the change in going from no time to time. But if time is infinite, that means an infinite amount of time had to pass in order to get us to the present moment. To get us here.* Here."

Here we are. Me and him, Jess below deck and Tommy at the wheel. Here we are, together, at the end of time. At the end of infinity.

I'm soaring. *Flying.* Up to join the stars. Far below, the boat, the lake, the earth.

How could I have overlooked it? They overlooked it, too, I think. The not-Romans. Perhaps we are the beginning and the end of all things. Perhaps we are the unlimited. Like that old Zen koan, what sound does a falling tree make in a deserted forest? Maybe, maybe what Socrates wants me to believe is the tree can't fall if nobody is there to see it, there can be no sound if nobody is there to hear it, and there can be no world, no universe, if nobody exists who can wonder at it all and get it all wrong and wonder some more, with a kidnapped baby, a son, *his* son in his arms.

*"Think about Descartes and his Meditations! He began his inquiry into the nature of reality with the words 'Cogito Ergo Sum.' 'I think therefore I am.' Metaphysics begins with* you, *Jack. You have no way of knowing for sure that the universe exists without you. You have no way of knowing* you *aren't its creator, and that everything in it isn't just a piece of* you."

Yes. Maybe what Socrates wants me to believe is that the world needs us as much as we need it. That the air needs to be breathed and the ground walked and the snow, snow needs to be flung in the shape of a ball at a friend's face. Could we be the ceiling to end all ceilings, could we be our own Golden Fleeces?

"Socrates—it's just—not like that. We're not that great. We're not that special. After this, there's just graduation and college and family that doesn't include you. Midlife crises and death from natural causes while hooked up to machines, surrounded by grandchildren and great-grand-children, who look on me like some ancient thing. . . ." My heart is heavy, so heavy—I want to fly but can't, my heart is dragging me down! Someday Socrates himself will be in a position exactly like this. I can do nothing for him. I can't save him from growing old and the land of the dead-and-dying any more than I could stop my own balls from dropping, my own voice from growing coarse.

My head reels from it all. I need to talk. To someone.

In the captain's cabin, Tommy's still at the wheel. "Tommy," I say. "Can't you drop an anchor or something? You should get some rest. Or something."

"Nah, dude, I'm fine. You guys all right? You were gone a while. Least it felt like a while. Not really sure."

"Jess is fine," I say. "Left her with a bear, I think. And Socrates and I—"

Tommy blinks. "You left Jess with a—"

"A bear," I say, impatiently. The boy *is* a bit drunk. He can't be blamed for slow uptake in this state.

"A bear," he repeats.

"A bear," I say.

"But, Jack, where did you get a bear?"

"Where did *you* get a bear?" I exclaim. As if I know anything about seafaring bears. Besides, it's his fricking ship. What makes me responsible for its bear population in the first place?

"Where did *I* get a bear?" Tommy says, and looks puzzled. "I don't know . . ."

"Look, man. The bear's not the important part."

"Man, I think the bear is pretty imp—"

"Forget the bear, Tommy! It's not about the bear at all. Socrates and I, we were walking around and I was telling him about where everything comes from. He thought everything comes from us, but I don't know if I can believe in that, Tommy, I just don't know, and then I thought about how we're going to get old and cruddy and he will, too, and I can't stop that, and what good's a father if he can't stop his son from growing old?"

He pauses. "So—so Socrates told you the meaning of life?"

Now's my turn to pause. "Something like that."

"But you don't buy it because you're going to get old and cruddy."

"Something like that."

"And you think you should be able to stop him from getting old and cruddy."

"Right," I say.

"But, Jack," he says, "I still think the bear is pretty important."

"Tommy, this is about more than the bear. There's more at stake here than the bear. The bear is like a grain of sand in, in"—I blank on the name of that big-ass desert in Africa—"in the big-ass desert in Africa."

"The Nubian?" Tommy says.

"No, not the Nubian."

"The Libyan one?"

"No, not the Libyan one."

"The—"

"Look, man, that's not what's important. The desert and the bear don't matter. It's all about Socrates growing old. Don't you see? How can a father let his son grow old?"

Tommy regards me a long time. "The Sahara?"

"Yeah," I say, relieved. "That's it."

"Okay," Tommy says. "I think I get what you're saying. When I thought you were talking about the Nubian you totally lost me, but now I think I know what you're saying."

I want to hug Tommy for knowing what I'm saying, but we're both somewhat drunk and he barely has any clothes on (*why is he in his underwear???*) so maybe now's not the best time. The last thing I need on top of everything else is a gay hookup with my best friend who's going away to get shot god-knows-where. Maybe later, though, once the whole kidnapping business has been sorted out. When he doesn't go on, I say, "*Well?*"

"Well," he says slowly. "Well, I mean, when has a father ever stopped his son from getting old? Just look at us. And Jess. And everyone else in the whole world. We're getting older and cruddier by the second."

"I know. But. Don't you think something's wrong with that?"

He doesn't answer right away.

"Don't you?"

"Man, I don't know. Yeah. I guess. Yeah. And maybe no, you know? It's like I told you before. With the quest thing. Except there's another side to it, too. I've been thinking and, well, yeah, the quest keeps you together, keeps you young, but, you know, the quest can't go on forever. It can't be never-ending. Where'd the meaning be in that shit? Where'd the point be in that? Because, man, if it went on forever, if the evil and the monsters kept coming and coming, then you'd only get a different kind of old and a different kind of separated and that would be as bad, you know?"

"Kind of," I say.

"But, Jack," he says, putting the engine in neutral, and turning to me.

"Yeah, man?"

"I think you're under-representing the importance of the bear."

We thud, thud, thud our way down the steps, Tommy in front, brandishing the mop that tried to attack him, and me bringing up the rear with Socrates. Our mission: Rescue Jess from the bear. Socrates and I are along primarily for auxiliary support of the moral order.

"Tommy," I whisper. "If the plan fails and the bear eats you and me and Jess, do you think it will adopt Socrates and raise him as a cub?"

"This isn't *The Jungle Book*, man," he says. "It would probably eat him for dessert."

Reaching the bottom of the stairs, we proceed slow and careful, my left hand on Tommy's shoulder, his broom tapping the ground like an epileptic blind man's cane. The only light seeps out of the bathroom. I head for it—deposit Socrates in his basket, still on the bathroom floor—and rejoin Tommy.

"What's all the noise?" Jess says in a sleepy voice.

"Jess," I say.

She's alive. She's—

"Don't run, Jess," Tommy says. "That'll make it chase you. And whatever you do, whatever you do, don't look the bear in the eye."

"What"—she hesitates—"are you talking about?"

"Shhhhh," Tommy says.

"You shush," Jess says.

"*Jess*," I say in as imploring a tone as I can.

"*Jack*," she says, mocking me. Then, "Oh my God."

"Jess?" I say.

"What is it?" Tommy says.

"I—I—I think I feel it."

"Where?" Tommy says.

"Where, Jess?" I say.

"I think—oh my God."

"What?" I say.

"I think I'm sitting on it."

"What do you mean, you're sitting on it?" Tommy hisses.

"I mean, I think I'm sitting on the bear."

"Hold on. Shhhhh," Tommy says.

We listen.

"I don't hear it breathing," Tommy says.

"Maybe it's hibernating," I suggest. I'm pretty sure I heard on the Discovery channel that the rate of breathing for a hibernating bear is like once a minute.

"Jack," Jess says.

"Yeah, Jess?" I say, tense.

"Don't be an idiot."

The bear does indeed turn out to be hibernating. That or dead. Kind of comfortable, too. Who knew bears could be so comfortable?

The nausea hits as soon as my eyes open. I'm on a couch covered with a furry blanket.

My head is heavy, my stomach empty, but I dry-gag

at the thought of ingesting food. Jess sits on the couch, watching me.

Socrates. Where is—

My heart races. I'm about to get up—but then, I'm *holding* him. I've *been* holding him. *Last night*—him crying, my having to get up in the middle of night, stumbling to the bathroom, searching for formula . . . I sigh. And again. I could've killed him. Could've rolled over on him a thousand times.

"We're here," Jess says. "Tommy says we're here. I'm— I'm sorry, Jack," she adds in a whisper.

I hold my son, and listen to his breathing. Listen to his dreams. And though I don't want to, I offer him to her, like I should have so many more times on this trip. She looks at me in surprise. I keep my arms outstretched.

She wants to take him just as badly as I want to keep him. I can see it in her eyes. She takes him. Now it's my turn to watch him dream in someone else's arms.

It hurts.

I leave them alone.

The sun's just started its ascent. Tommy's in the cabin, lying on the white couch by the wheel and staring up at the ceiling. Beyond the windshield is the familiar sight of

Clifford's small harbor covered in an early morning haze.

"Hey," he says.

"Hey," I say.

There's an awkward silence, which Tommy breaks by saying, "So what do you remember of last night? For some reason I keep thinking about bears in the Sahara searching for the meaning of life."

"I don't even know, man," I say.

The silence resumes. The horizon brightens.

Finally, I say, "Next time, Tommy, we'll stick to the road, I think."

He grins sheepishly and says, "So there's going to be a next time?"

# 11

## To Grandma's House with Socrates

The hum of tires on concrete serves as the soundtrack to the climax of our quest. I'm in the middle of the cab, Tommy's leaning against the right window, and Jess looks out the left, Socrates in her arms. We pass the cemetery where Grandpa is buried, where Bob will be buried, the graves solemn in the morning mist. We pass the now abandoned elementary school where they met. A breeze gently rocks a pair of rotting wooden swings in a playground littered with broken beer bottles.

Bob's house is an old cottage at the end of an unpaved road. A car is parked in the driveway—the home attendant's, probably. Mom and Dad wanted to set up Bob in a nice nursing home when she was first diagnosed, but she made them promise not to. She said the only way to fight her disease was to stay home.

We pay the cabbie, who whispers, "Thank you, enjoy your visit," and watch him drive off. Then I walk up a chipped brick walkway to the door of 7 Birch Street. I take a deep breath. Could turn back. I don't have to face Bob—whatever's left of her.

"I wish I wasn't so goddamn hung over," I say.

A hand on my shoulder—Tommy's. Jess leans in from the other side, brushes my cheek with her lips, and puts Socrates into my arms.

"We got your back," Tommy says.

"Yeah," Jess says. "Something like that."

I nod, and knock. Approaching footsteps . . . The door opens, revealing Mrs. Vandersloot, a tall, thin woman who smiles in a way that resembles a frown. She takes us in without much surprise, and says to me, "Jack? Is that you? But what are you doing here?"

"Just wanted to visit my Bob," I say. When she looks at me, uncomprehending, I say, "My grandma, I mean."

Mrs. Vandersloot actually frowns now, and says,

"I'm not sure so many visitors is a good idea, but—well, come in."

On Mrs. Vandersloot's insistence, I go in to see Bob alone. She's rocking slowly, almost imperceptibly in an old, creaky armchair, her walker off to the side. Looking at her is like looking into a mirror in the future—we have the same soft facial features, the same nose. *The nose I've passed onto Socrates.*

"Yosik?" she asks. My heart falls. She hasn't called me Yosik in years. She squints at me as I approach and I settle on the sofa next to her.

"Yes, Bob. I'm here."

"Oh, Yosik, I'm glad. So very glad. I told my friends that your parents were dropping you off today, and they were all jealous. So very jealous. You know how old ladies can be." She smiles at me in a way she hasn't smiled at me in many years. She's wearing a dress with lilies on it, one of those old lady dresses that depress the fuck out of you when you see them hanging in stores.

"While I was waiting for you I was thinking . . . Do you remember—it must've been a summer or two ago—do you remember how you showed me your secret place and made me promise not to tell anyone?"

"Yes," I say, and take a deep breath.

My secret place. A little clearing in the woods out back that I haven't thought of in years. As a kid, I imagined the surrounding trees were the beginning of a great and terrible forest.

"I wanted to visit it so very much, but these old legs—" she casts a quick, disapproving glance down at them. "And that *beastly* contraption," she says, by which I take her to mean her walker. "It's a beautiful place," she continues. "A most beautiful place. The kind of place where stories begin and end. Where little boys and girls fight trolls and witches and meet fairies and go on all sorts of adventures." She turns to me. "Can you tell me of an adventure you had there?"

I close my eyes and try to go back. Go back to when I stood there with her, and answered that very question. But I can't. Too much time has passed. So I tell her a new story. "Once upon a time, there was a kid named Yosik. Except he wasn't really even a kid anymore. He was at that age where—it's like, he's not quite a kid but not quite not-a-kid—"

She nods at me, encouragingly, and so I continue. "—and he had these friends, and they're all about to move away. So they go on this road trip together. This crazy road trip. And at the end, they get to Yosik's grandma's house, but nothing's really changed. They're still all going to move away. Nothing's really changed."

"Oh, Yosik," she says when I finish. "The friends you have in childhood you keep forever, no matter how old you get or where you go. They are a part of you."

"But how do you let go?"

She whispers to me, "By holding on as tight as you can. Even when they are beyond your reach."

And I whisper back, "Would you like to meet them?"

We sit in a circle around the kitchen table, the window open wide behind Bob. Bob is apologizing for not making any blintzes. "I don't know what's gotten into me! All I could think was you were coming and I forgot the most important thing of all! I'm so very sorry. I will make it up to you, I promise."

"It's okay, Bob," I say, biting my lip. "These—these are my friends. The ones I was telling you about. Tommy and Jess. And this"—I gesture to Socrates, on the floor in his basket—"is my—son. Your great-grandson. He—he has your nose."

She studies Socrates for a long time, until finally she breaks into a smile. "He does. He does have my nose, doesn't he?"

"Yes," I say.

"And it is for him—for him and your friends that you have gone on this adventure, Yosik?"

"Not just for them, Baba. For you, too. You're moving away, too. I wanted to say good-bye."

She does a thing I do not expect. She laughs. She laughs and says, "Then say good-bye, Yosik. Say good-bye! So many people in this world do not get to say good-bye. Their adventures go unresolved. But you have a chance to make everything come together. To write your own ending. Isn't that beautiful?"

"Yes, Baba," I say. "That is beautiful."

So I write my ending with Grandma. "Good-bye, Bob. Thank you for all the hundreds of blintzes and the stories and our summers together. And for my name. Thank you for giving me a new name, when I wanted it." I hesitate. "I'm sorry I didn't visit you more. I should've visited you more."

"Life would be a bore if we always did the things we should, wouldn't it?" She winks at me. "Good-bye, Yosik.

Thank you for choosing my house to run away to. It will always be here for you."

That last part stings, because I know it's not true.

I turn to Jess. I may never see her again, she'll probably graduate college and get a job and date someone who doesn't kidnap babies in his spare time. I say, "Thank you, Jess." It takes everything I have not to avert my gaze. "For every one of those horrible parties we went to. For hating beer with me. For listening to me talk about Nietzsche and eternal return whenever I got drunk. And for just being generally pretty awesome, even at the soon-to-be Olympic sport of shot-putting chairs. And, you know, for Socrates."

She brushes her hair out of her eyes and says, "Jack, I'm sorry for tossing that chair at you. Multiple times. You did deserve it—multiple times—but I *am* sorry."

Tommy's next and he knows it.

"Thank you—"

"Shut up, man. Don't look at me like that. This isn't the end."

"But if it is—"

"We'll be cellmates in jail, Jack. And when we get out we'll kidnap lots more babies. It'll be a ball."

"But if we don't—"

"We will."

"But if we don't, Tommy," I say. He doesn't interrupt this time. "If we don't, thanks for playing video games with me when I got my appendix out and for sticking with me even when you thought I'd kidnapped a dead philosopher after"—I hesitate, Bob is right there, but blurt it out anyway—"even when you thought I'd kidnapped a dead philosopher after sucking him off."

He sighs and says, "Man . . . anytime. What are dead philosophers for, anyway?"

Through the window I see a police car pull up.

Right on cue.

"Police," I say, and rise.

This is it. The gates have fallen. The city is lost.

I grab Socrates from the basket, look from Bob to Jess to Tommy.

Mrs. Vandersloot enters the kitchen, yells, "What are you doing?"

Everyone else yells, "Go!"

I go. Through the backyard. Down the road. Past a bunch of houses that have great big Manson Realtors "For Sale" signs in their front yards. Up and over the hill. Sneakers pounding, following in the footsteps of a little

Yosik, along the same shitty road I used to ride my tricycle and then my bike on when I came to visit in the summers, until the summer I told my parents I wanted to go to camp with my friends instead. The cemetery's on my right. I race past graves. They are black and they are gray and they are white. They are great marble blocks and unimposing slabs of granite.

And then—*the ending*.

I know how our story ends.

I rush through the metal gates, still wet from dew, past dozens of neglected graves. I almost miss Grandpa's marker. I barely remember him anymore. Just his beard. The beard might be from the pictures though, might not be a real memory.

Next to Grandpa's marker is a plot Bob picked out for herself.

Elena Yevgenivna Kamenovskaya 1936–

I stop, gasping for breath.

Here. The entirety of time up to this point has brought us *here*.

I hold Socrates, and wait for enlightenment.

A police siren wails.

Time. No time. The Fates are coming. This is his third day.

The crunching of footsteps.

Quickly. Off with the chains and out of the cave! We must step out and fly. Away from the Fates. Away from an incomprehensible universe. Away into enlightenment.

"Sir. Sir. Please hand over the baby. Sir."

With Socrates in my hands, I jump.

Air beneath my feet.

The sky above.

The sun, bright. Hot.

The temporary elation of flight.

But the chains pull us down.

"Sir. What are you doing? Sir . . ."

Once more I try. Once more I fall.

*"But—but in falling, we fly, don't we? We fly vertically. That's the paradox of vertical flight. Falling is the only way we can fly."*

My stomach, my chest, are all in knots.

*"Even if we cast off the chains, we would fly too close to the sun. We would burn our wings and fall anyway."*

The last thing I say to Socrates before they take him from me is, *"Do svedanya."* It is Russian for "good-bye," or more literally, "Till we meet again."

# Epilogue

What a few hours ago I might have taken for the coming of the second great flood—a rain to drown the world in—has given way to drizzle, mist, and that old, hollow calm all storms leave in their wake. We look out at puddles and wet pavement and ashen skies in silence. Eventually, I force my eyes away, back inside, to the check lying on our table. I pick it up. The cost of our graduation dinner adds up to $30.60.

Thirty-sixty.

He hasn't said a word. Just keeps looking out the window.

I clear my throat and say, "Would you like something else, maybe? Another milkshake? I think I'll have a milk-shake myself. Been a while since I had one. Do you—do you want to join me?"

He meets my eye then, and with a quiet smile says, "Sure." And I am so happy. I am so happy he wants another goddamn milkshake.

I wave the waitress over, explain we're not quite done yet. We'd like two milkshakes. A vanilla and—I glance at him and he says chocolate, so I turn back to her and say chocolate and she nods. I feel suddenly guilty for us keeping her here, with the place empty, tell her we're celebrating a graduation. She says she knows. She says she'll be right out with the milkshakes.

"Well, aren't you going to finish?" he asks.

"What do you mean?"

"The story," he says in a tone that implies I'm slow. "I thought that's why you wanted to stay longer. To finish."

"I thought I had. Finished."

"Then give me the epilogue," he says with a slight upturn of his upper-right lip. He does that sometimes. I even have a few pictures of him and that cheeky half-grin of his.

"Okay," I sigh. "Well . . . things got pretty ugly for a little while. But your—" I hesitate. "Your parents, they took pity on me. Jess thought it would be better to just move on. Let you go. But I—couldn't. All I asked was that I could still see you. That they would let me see you."

I hear the tap of the waitress's heels. She sets our shakes on the table and says, "Take your time."

He waits until she's gone before he asks, "And what did you see?"

"Sorry?"

"What did you see? Haven't you ever read a good epilogue?"

"Well, sure—"

"Soooo?"

"So. So I saw your first birthday, which I spent sitting very awkwardly in the corner of your parents' home and occasionally walking over to you and whispering in your ear about philosophy's worst enemy, the infinite regress. Then I went off on a tangent and introduced you to the liar's paradox."

He raises an eyebrow, so I explain. "Everything I say is a lie. If when I said 'everything I say is a lie' I was lying, then I was telling the truth about always lying, but if I was telling the truth about always lying, then I wasn't lying, and so I wasn't telling the truth about always lying. And so on."

He screws his face up into a look of intense concentration. Eventually, he says, "I think my head is going to explode."

I gesture at the napkins. "We can pick up some of those heavy-duty Bounty ones on the way back. If you want to be a philosopher you'll need them. Nothing cleans up after an infinite regress like Bounty."

"You should've gone into advertising."

I nod.

"That reminds me," he says. "I was baby-sitting my neighbor's kid the other day and he just kept asking me 'why,' 'why,' 'why'? We started off on why he has to go to school and a few minutes later I was arguing that human beings need to diversify labor in order to have the leisure time to develop culture and create art. Eventually we got into the metaphysics. I argued we live in a clockwork universe, with everything being causally determined."

"How old was he?"

"Five."

I laugh.

He bends over his milkshake and sips. I watch the whipped cream peeking out of his glass slip from view, gulp by gulp. When he looks up at me, he's wearing a whipped cream mustache. "I wish I could remember," he says. "The quest. Like you wanted me to."

"Nobody remembers those years," I say.

"Was it hard for you?" he asks. "Me not knowing?"

"Well. Yeah. Easy and hard, I guess."

"Are you really going Anaximander on me? Now?"

"Not Anaximander," I say. "More along the lines of Heraclitus. For Anaximander, hard and easy would be constantly alternating, never existing at the same time," and I wave my hands in a gesture for an eternal cycle of opposites coming into being and perishing. "But Heraclitus, Heraclitus knows they're both distinct parts of a single unified whole." The hands come together and stay together. "Simultaneously, easy and hard. The easy part being I didn't have to pay for your short-lived piano lessons, for starters."

He rolls his eyes. "What do you do when it gets hard though? Think about jumping out of windows?" He's joking, I know, but also not.

"No," I say. "I have no wings, you see. No wings. How do men get by without wings?"

"By flapping their arms and pretending while hurtling toward the ground at terminal velocity?"

"By flapping their wings and *flying*," I say with a wry smile.

"Just to clarify. Flying *toward* the ground?"

I nod. "Toward the ground."

"I'm starting to think you might really be a romantic."

"Oh, you have no idea," I say, and sigh. "For a long time I tried to be a cynic, but, smoke and mirrors, all of it. I have a theory about how we all are. Deep down."

"Or you could be making a generalization about all of humanity based on your own subjective disposition."

"Or that. But I don't think so. I mean, look." I lean back in my seat. "We'll never really know *anything* for certain. There's always more 'why's, more questions. We don't know that life has meaning. That this isn't all a dream. That we won't get splattered by one of the many pianos you never learned to play falling out of the sky the moment we step outside. But we've got to *believe*. In something. In *each other.* Otherwise, what's the point of you and me, sitting here? I still haven't taken the leap on the whole God question, but on those days when it's hard, for one reason or another, I try to have faith in *people.* In *me* and *you* and

*Tommy* and *Jess* and *Bob* and even one or two folks I've met in my post-baby-napping years."

With that, I set myself upon my milkshake. Halfway through, I pause long enough to say, "Diners really do have good milkshakes."

"Told you," he says.

I pay the check, and soon we're in my car, driving through wet, dark, and cold back to his parents'—*adopted parents'*—house, with only the streetlamps and traffic lights and shadows in the night to guide us. Just as we pull into the driveway he asks, "You ever see Jess again?"

"Yeah. We'd go out for lunch. After college, though, she moved out west for a job, Oregon I think, and I kind of lost track of her."

"Oh . . . What about Tommy? You ever get to be cell-mates in prison?

I laugh. "No. No, we did not. Sometimes I wish we had. Gone to the same jail. Gone to the same college. Done the same something."

"You're not close anymore?"

The way he says it, I know exactly what he wants. He wants to know what happens to friends whose lives are pushed apart.

"I still see him here and there. When he's on leave. I don't always know why. Sometimes I think it's just sheer momentum. He's bulkier, taller now. Not as funny. Has a balding spot on the back of his head. But a few hours into dinner, after more than a few drinks, after we've cleared away all the bullshit, there are moments when I forget how old he is and he forgets how old I am, and it's like we're still those kids, sitting together in the cafeteria, sharing hot fries."

He nods. "I—I think I have friends like that," he says. "Who I've known for such a long time I don't know what's keeping us together anymore. Do—do all friends end up that way?"

He sounds too old. Much too old. When did he get this old?

"I don't know. But I have to believe that there's truth in whatever keeps drawing us back to our friends. Whatever keeps us together. I think that's worth making a leap of faith for."

"Even if you're *leaping* out of a plane and the ground is forty thousand feet below?"

I stop to consider. I'm not fond of planes, those goddamned usurpers.

"Yeah," I say.

"Even if you end up hitting the ground at terminal velocity?"

What is this boy's fixation on hitting the ground at terminal velocity? "There are worse reasons to," I say. "Just about every other reason is worse."

"If you say so," he says, and though the car lights have gone off by now, I imagine him with his right lip upturned and despite myself, reach forward and tousle his hair in the darkness.

"Sorry," I say. "Couldn't resist. You—you should probably get going now."

"Yeah," he says. "Would you like to come in? Have some tea?"

I would, but I say, "No, no, I've got to get going, too. Long way home and all."

"All right. Goodnight. And thanks," he says, getting out of the car.

"*Do svedanya*," I say.

"*Do svedanya*," he says, and pushes the door shut. I watch him walk up the porch, ring the bell, give me a wave, and disappear into his house. I sit there for a few minutes, by myself, and regret not telling him. Not telling him that I know his favorite cereal is Honey Nut Cheerios, and I know he doesn't want to learn to drive because he doesn't want to risk running anyone over. I know that while he argued for a clockwork universe to a five-year-old, he also thinks "dogs are good people" and admits "I guess that means I think they have free will." I know he's terrified of growing up and losing his friends, just as I am of losing him. But we still have time. Time before college and a career, marriage and kids. And where there's some time, there's all time.